The
Tree of Bells

The
Tree of Bells

JEAN THESMAN

Houghton Mifflin Company
Boston 1999

The text of this book is set in 13-point Garamond No. 3.

Library of Congress Cataloging-in-Publication Data

Thesman, Jean.
The tree of bells / Jean Thesman.
p. cm.
Sequel to: The ornament tree.
Summary: While living in a boardinghouse managed by her
mother and grandmother in Seattle in 1922, sixteen-year-
old Clare decides her future at a time of limited opportunities
for women.
ISBN 0-395-90510-9
[1. Boardinghouse — Fiction. 2. Interpersonal
relations — Fiction.] I. Title.
PZ7.T3525Tr 1999
[Fic] — dc21 98-27787
CIP AC

Printed in the United States of America

BP 10 9 8 7 6 5 4 3 2 1

This is for Christine White

1

"New Year's Eve is only two days away, Bonnie," Clare Harris told her cousin. "You should be here with us to see 1922 come in. It would mean so much to everyone, especially if they knew that you won't be —"

"But they *won't* know," Bonnie Shaster said urgently as she pulled a knitted cap over her short blond hair. "You must keep my secret, Clare. Promise you won't tell the others until I'm ready for them to know."

"I've already promised," Clare said. She laughed a little, and blinked to keep tears from her dark blue eyes. "But I wish you hadn't told me. It's too big a secret. Everyone will be so upset. And *he* —"

"Shh." Bonnie looked over her shoulder to see if anyone was coming. "I'm glad he didn't get back in time. If I'd seen him again, I'm not sure I could have left without telling him something."

1

They stood close together in the front hall of the boarding house, speaking in whispers. The door was open, and a blast of winter air blew through.

Bonnie's suitcases waited on the porch. She had dressed warmly for the short ride to the train station, wearing the old coat she had saved for her trips home to Seattle. The mild weather in Berkeley, California, where she attended college, was much more to her liking.

Clare reached out suddenly and hugged her. "I'm nearly sixteen, and I'm taller than you are now, Bonnie. That must count for something! No, don't laugh. I'm asking you again — please *please* tell Grandmother what you're going to do."

Bonnie smiled and tugged gently on Clare's smooth brown braids. "Telling Audra would be a mistake. You know how she's going to react."

"Then tell Winnie," Clare urged. "She's always eager for adventure. She'll appreciate what you're planning even if I can't."

Bonnie kissed Clare's cheek and stepped back. "I hear Mr. Reynolds' auto coming," she said. "It's time to say good-bye."

From the foot of the stairs, she called out, "Audra? Sally? Winnie? Who's coming to the station with me?"

"Is it time?" Clare's elegant grandmother, Audra Devereaux, appeared at the head of the stairs, smoothing her silver-gilt braids. "Is Mr. Reynolds here already?"

Mr. Reynolds was the only boarder who owned an auto, and at breakfast he had offered to take Bonnie and her relatives to the station. During the young widower's years at the boarding house, he had come to think of the Devereaux women as his own relatives.

Clare looked out the open door, then reported to her grandmother that Mr. Reynolds had parked in front of the house and was hurrying toward the porch.

"I'll be downstairs immediately," Audra said, and she disappeared, only to reappear a moment later carrying her coat, gloves, and pocketbook. "You have your ticket, Bonnie?" she asked. "Your pocket money?"

Bonnie nodded. "I haven't left anything behind," she said.

"I wish you were leaving *yourself* behind with us," Winnie Devereaux said as she hurried downstairs. She was a cousin of Audra's long-dead husband, and had lived in the big Devereaux house for more than thirty years. "I hate saying good-bye to you whenever you leave, and at the same time I envy you for what you're doing. But you'll be home again in June."

Clare and Bonnie exchanged a quick, guilty look.

Audra, whose clear gray eyes missed nothing, said, "Is something wrong, girls?" She had been pulling on her kid gloves, and she stopped to study her granddaughter and Bonnie, the girl who had been left in her care after her parents had died years before.

"Nothing's wrong, Grandmother," Clare said firmly. "Is Mama going with you to the station? She had better come down right away."

"She's decided to go straight to the library, and that's in the opposite direction," Winnie said. She wrapped herself in the black wool cape she favored on cold days and yanked a felt hat down low over her iron-gray hair. "She didn't think she should take off the whole day. And what about you, Clare? Mr. Reynolds' car is large enough for all of us. Won't you change your mind and come?"

Clare bit her lip, then said, "I've already said my good-byes. Bonnie understands."

Her grandmother gave her a strange look, and Clare blushed under the scrutiny. She would have a hard time keeping Bonnie's secret plans for the future. Everyone in the house loved her, and they all wanted to know every detail of her life.

Bonnie had asked Clare not to go to the station. She suspected that Mr. Younger, who had boarded with them for several years, would stay away to avoid saying good-bye, and she did not want him returning to an empty, lonely house.

Mr. Reynolds, young and dark and, in the opinion of Clare and her friends, devastatingly handsome, stuck his head in the open door and said, "I'm leaving for the station immediately, although I can't imagine why, since I'm not going anywhere. If any of you ladies want to ride with me — and that includes Miss Bonnie Shaster herself — then you had better get out to the auto right this minute."

They laughed at him, as he meant them to do, and Clare's mother, Sally Harris, hearing the laughter, ran through the hall from the kitchen, carrying a small cardboard box tied with string. "I nearly missed you, Bonnie!" she exclaimed.

"I didn't know you were in the kitchen, Mama," Clare said. "What were you doing?"

"Fixing a special lunch," Sally said, handing the box to Bonnie. "Mrs. Klacker asked me to do it before she left for the market. She was afraid she wouldn't be back in time because the roads are so bad and the streetcars run late in weather like this."

"Ladies, ladies," Mr. Reynolds said in a protesting voice as he consulted his gold pocket watch. "Are we going or are we staying?"

Sally kissed Bonnie, Clare hugged her once more, and Mr. Reynolds ushered them out the door. "I've known chickens that were easier to herd," he complained, holding out his arms to Winnie and Audra when they reached the slippery steps.

"You've never known a chicken personally in your entire life, you young snob," Winnie said, taking his arm.

"Please do not quarrel on the porch," Audra said. She proceeded majestically down the steps, her gloved fingers barely touching Mr. Reynolds' arm. "The neighbors have enough to talk about."

"Oh, wait!" Bonnie exclaimed. She pulled a narrow strip of white paper out of her pocket and hurried around to the side yard. Clare knew where she was going.

She followed and watched from a distance while Bonnie tied the strip of paper to a bare branch of the Ornament Tree, the old apple tree where Devereaux women had fastened their wishes and hopes for nearly forty years. Two other strips fluttered in the cold wind, one Clare had put there herself on the day Bonnie told her the secret and the other tied there by someone else. No one ever looked at anyone else's strip of paper. When the papers had weathered and finally blown away, perhaps everyone's wishes and hopes would come true.

Bonnie had known Clare was watching. "Now I can leave and have peace of mind," she told her cousin.

"I hope you didn't make a wish that will make me cry," Clare said.

Bonnie laughed. "You know you aren't supposed to even wonder what I wished."

She was right. Clare walked around to the front of the house again, hugging herself against the cold, and went inside.

Her mother stood in the bay window in the front parlor, watching the auto leave. Clare, struggling with tears, sat down at the table where the boarders played bridge in the evenings, and she stared miserably at the intricate inlaid top.

"There they go," Sally said. She let the lace curtains drop back in place. "I don't know whether to be glad or sorry that the snow began melting when it did. It would have been nice if we could have kept Bonnie with us a few more days. But then, there's always so much to do, getting ready for classes after the long Christmas break. You'll see, Clare, when you start college."

Clare, twisting her fingers together so hard that they hurt, said, "But I won't be going to college in California, Mama. I'm not like Bonnie. I —" She nearly choked on her tears.

Sally stared at her. "What's wrong? I know you miss her when she's gone, but —"

Clare shook her head. "Nothing's wrong, Mama," she said. "It's just — I don't know. Winter, perhaps. Some years it seems to go on forever."

Sally smoothed Clare's bangs away from her forehead. "We haven't even reached January yet. And this morning Mrs. Klacker said we're in for a big storm."

"Her bunions told her so," Clare said, laughing unwillingly. The boarders regarded the cook's feet as uncanny predictors of Seattle's weather.

"Walk with me to the library," Sally said suddenly. "Getting out for half an hour will do you good, and if Mrs. Klacker doesn't get home in time, you can heat up the leftover soup for your lunch. And give some to Mr. Younger, too, if he comes home." She frowned a little. "Isn't it strange that he didn't come back to tell Bonnie good-bye?"

"Mama, for heaven's sake," Clare said. "Bonnie comes and goes all the time. He can't be expected to leave the school in horrible weather like this and rush home because she's going back to college again."

"He likes her," her mother said. "Has she ever said anything to you about him?"

"She only cares about school," Clare said. "And don't forget that Mr. Reynolds likes her, too. Men are always crazy about Bonnie."

Her mother nodded. "Because she hardly notices them," she said.

Clare was anxious to end the conversation. She consulted her small gold wristwatch, a Christmas gift from

Grandmother. It was possible that Mr. Younger might come home for lunch. Sometimes he did, if he wasn't involved with afternoon classes at the school for the blind. But from his expression when he left that morning, Clare scarcely knew what to expect. He'd been so upset.

Mr. Younger loved Bonnie, Clare thought. He had encouraged her to grow and dream, but how would he feel when he learned where her dreams were taking her?

"All right, Mama, I'll come with you," Clare said. "You're probably right. I need a walk."

"And when you get back, perhaps Marietta can come over," Sally said. Clare knew her mother was doing her best to sound reassuring.

"Marietta had to see the dentist this morning," Clare said. "She won't feel like going anywhere. But I've got my Christmas books to keep me busy, and there's the new piece for the piano."

Her mother's lightly freckled face was drawn with worry. "It's that letter you got from your father, isn't it?" she asked. "I wish he'd leave you alone."

Clare shook her head. "No, it's not the letter, Mama. I know better than to take him seriously. He won't keep his promise to send money or pay for my schooling — it's just talk. That's all he ever does. I only hope that he stays away from me."

"He's afraid of your grandmother," Sally said. "Don't

worry that he'll show up. Now get your coat and walk with me. I want to see some color in your pale face."

The library was only a few blocks from the Devereaux house on Crescent Road. The bitter weather and abrupt thaw had caused the sidewalks to crack and heave up in several places, and as they passed one intersection, they saw a work crew shoveling gravel into a gaping hole in the street.

One of the workers, a small boy in a thin jacket, glanced toward Clare and her mother as they crossed the intersection, and a man, seeing his attention distracted from the work, cuffed him hard enough to knock off his ragged cloth cap.

Sally sighed. "Look at that child," she said. "I should call the city and complain about his working out here in the cold, but they would just say that he's on his Christmas holiday so he's not missing school, and besides, a little hard work is good for a boy. Sometimes I think it's hopeless, trying to protect children from the people who exploit them."

Clare looked back at the boy, who was struggling with a bucket of gravel. He could not have been more than eight or nine years old, and he was wearing a man's old boots.

"Maybe he brought a lunch to someone and they're letting him help out," she said, more to comfort her mother than because she believed what she was saying. "If he's still here when I get back, I'll tell Winnie. She'll do something about it."

Winnie was not afraid of anything. She and Audra had been leaders in the movement to achieve voting rights for women. They were active volunteers in the Neighborhood House, a place where poor women and girls could go to receive job training and information on health and child care. And, to Clare's discomfort, they distributed pamphlets explaining birth control. Every time they did it, they risked arrest and imprisonment. Not even a doctor could discuss birth control with a patient.

Clare said good-bye to her mother on the front steps of the library, then turned to hurry home. The work crew was still there when she reached the intersection, but the boy was sitting on the curb, holding a dirty sleeve to his bleeding nose and sobbing bitterly. He looked up when Clare approached him, his light blue eyes filled with despair, then he looked down again as if to hide his thoughts from her.

"Are you all right?" Clare asked him. She had seen blood smeared over his face and dripping off his chin, and she was horrified, but she tried hard to keep her voice calm.

The boy did not answer, but only buried his face into

the crook of his arm. His sobbing stopped, and Clare could see his shoulders heave with the effort to keep silent. She knelt beside him, the hem of her wool coat dragging in the slush, and touched his knee.

"Let me see your face," she said. "I won't hurt you."

"You git away from that kid!" a man shouted at her.

Clare stepped back in alarm. A short, stocky man rushed at her, his unshaven face twisted with anger.

"Whatchoo want with that kid?" he yelled.

"He's hurt," Clare said. Her voice sounded weak and frightened, even to her.

The man took advantage of her fear and stepped so close to her that she could smell the whiskey on his breath. He was filthy. His face and chapped hands were grimy, and his clothes were black with grease and dirt.

"You get away from the kid," he said. "Leave him alone."

Clare backed away and nearly lost her balance. The boy looked up then, his dirty, bloody face anguished.

"Let me alone, please, Miss," he begged.

Clare turned and ran. What was wrong with everyone? You stopped and tried to help, and someone attacked you. How could Grandmother and Winnie go on and on with the work they did?

But the boy's eyes would haunt her for a long time, she knew.

She had been home only long enough to hang up her coat when she heard the streetcar stop at the corner. Mr. Younger would not be on this one, she thought. He would not take the chance of coming home and finding Bonnie still there. But she went to look out the window anyway, and there he was, climbing down the streetcar steps carefully while stout Mrs. Klacker waited on the icy sidewalk.

Mrs. Klacker put down one of her shopping bags and reached out to touch Mr. Younger's arm. Clare saw him brush her hand aside while he tested the ground with the tip of his white cane. Mrs. Klacker reached out again and grasped his arm firmly. Mr. Younger gave up and let her guide him to a safe patch of sidewalk. Then she went back for her shopping bag. Mr. Younger tapped his way along and turned when the tip of his cane told him that he had reached the walk that led to the porch.

Mrs. Klacker followed behind, watching him. Clare knew how frustrated she must feel. Mr. Younger hated to have anyone attempt to help him.

She opened the door for them and made certain Mr. Younger knew she was there by speaking first.

"Here you are," she said. "I only got home a moment

ago, so I'm afraid you'll have to wait a bit for your tea."

The sight of his lean, sober face always had the same effect on her, and she hated the blush that stung her cheeks and the way her voice trembled a little when she spoke to him.

"Oh, I'll fix his tea," Mrs. Klacker said as she puffed up the steps behind the blind man. "I'll fix his tea and his soup at the same time, and warm him up for lunch. I've got this nice bit of salmon I'll poach for him later, don't you worry, Clare."

Mr. Younger wore glasses with black lenses, and Clare suspected that he thought they hid his emotions. But he was wrong. His face revealed everything. Now Clare read sadness and annoyance both, and she was sorry.

"You had a bad morning, didn't you?" she asked him as Mrs. Klacker hurried away to the kitchen.

"I've had worse," he grumbled. "I just can't remember when." He took off his hat and brushed back his fair hair, then fumbled a little while he hung his coat on the rack in the front hall. Clare didn't help him. She knew better.

"Bonnie's gone?" he asked abruptly.

"Yes," she said. "Grandmother and Winnie went along, and they'll stop by the Neighborhood House on the way back, so there'll only be the two of us at lunch."

"Your mother's at the library?" he asked as he stalked

14

through the dining room toward his lair, the small side parlor where he always ate his meals alone.

Clare followed, as she usually did. "Yes, I walked her there. And on the way back—" She stopped. She had been about to tell him about the boy, but the mere thought of him upset her. And that awful, dirty man!

"Yes, yes?" Mr. Younger said impatiently as he sat in his favorite chair facing the window he could not see. "On the way back—what? You saw Rudolph Valentino?"

Clare shook her head angrily. Oh, he was so exasperating! She and her best friend, Marietta Nelson, had made the mistake of telling him how much they had enjoyed the movie, *The Sheik,* which starred the dramatically handsome actor, and Mr. Younger had taken heartless pleasure in reminding them of their confession over and over again.

"If I had, you may be sure I'd have lunch with him instead of you," Clare said pertly.

He sighed impatiently. "I can't understand you and your friend. Don't you have something better to do with your time? Can you imagine Bonnie wasting even an hour watching silly motion pictures?"

Clare scowled and blurted, "Bonnie and Elena wrote a letter to Mr. Valentino, and he sent them a photograph of himself. He even autographed it."

15

"My god," Mr. Younger breathed. "Well, why not? Elena wants to be an actress. Isn't that correct? Give Bonnie another year in California, and she'll change her mind about being a physician. The next thing we hear about her, she'll be one of those Boop-a-Doop girls, dancing all night and drinking bathtub gin cocktails with gangsters."

Clare burst out laughing unwillingly, and then sobered. If he knew what Bonnie was really planning, he would prefer her dancing all night with gangsters. She would be safer.

"Well, well?" Mr. Younger grouched. "Are you just going to stand there or are you going to read the morning paper to me?"

"Heavens, but you're cranky today!" Clare exclaimed, but she ran for the paper and read to him until Mrs. Klacker brought in his lunch tray.

"Your lunch is ready in the dining room," the woman told Clare. "I found a bit of that cheese you like, Clare."

"I do not want cheese!" Mr. Younger said.

"I haven't given *you* cheese, you disagreeable child!" Mrs. Klacker answered. "I never give you cheese. Stop fussing and eat your soup."

"Not until the two of you leave the room," Mr. Younger said, scowling. Clare knew he was self-conscious, afraid of appearing clumsy when he ate.

16

Mrs. Klacker took Clare's arm and they left the room. "He's a terrible bear of a man," Mrs. Klacker muttered when Clare sat down at the long table. "Only Bonnie cheers him up. Bonnie and Mrs. Devereaux."

But I don't, Clare thought with despair. Even when he learns that she won't be back for a long time, he won't smile at me.

Bonnie was not the only one with a secret.

2

Before the afternoon passed, a wild storm swept over Seattle, bending trees and sending small branches clattering against the windows in the fine old house. Grandmother and Winnie returned shortly after it began, laughing and windblown, their arms full of papers and books.

"How was everything at the Neighborhood House?" Clare asked as she helped her grandmother out of her coat. She was both fascinated and repelled by the women's volunteer work with the city's poorest women and children.

"We're doing wonderfully well with the child care classes," she said. "We —"

Through the howl of the wind, they heard another, more ominous sound. Outside, something was cracking and grinding, and finally they heard a great, heavy thud.

"Oh, a tree's down!" Winnie cried.

"Which one was it?" Grandmother asked as she hurried from window to window in the large front parlor.

"It sounded as if it was at the side of the house, Audra," Winnie said.

They saw it finally, through the window of the smaller second parlor. The Ornament Tree lay twisted and broken on the lawn.

Grandmother pressed her hand against her mouth and turned away from the window.

"Now, now, Audra," Winnie said. "Don't start thinking it means bad luck or something silly like that."

Mrs. Klacker bustled through the hall door. "Mr. Younger wants to know what happened."

"The Ornament Tree's down, but don't tell him!" Clare said. Sometimes he tied wishes to the tree, wishes he had printed painstakingly and alone in his room. He would not admit it, but Clare knew that he, like the Devereaux women, believed in the power of the old tree.

"What am I supposed to say?" Mrs. Klacker asked. "I don't want to lie to the man."

"I'll tell him," Grandmother said quietly. She left the room quickly, her face pale.

"Who would believe we put so much faith in an old superstition?" Winnie asked. "Stars and bars, we're modern women. We ought to be ashamed of ourselves."

"So you say," Mrs. Klacker said. "But haven't I seen you going out after dark to plead your own case when you thought no one was watching?"

"Hush," Winnie said. Her face flushed darkly. "You're not our nanny."

"There are some who might question that," Mrs. Klacker said, and she disappeared in the direction of the kitchen, laughing to herself.

Winnie stared out the window at the fallen tree and finally said, "I'll call the yard man to come and clear it away tomorrow. Look, Clare. I can see three strips of paper. Should we take them off?"

Goose bumps raised on Clare's arms. "Maybe we should, before the yard man comes. He might look."

"You're right," Winnie said. She was biting her lower lip, and Clare wondered if the third strip had been hers.

Clare pulled on her raincoat and ran outside. The wind was still wild, and the bare branches of the fallen tree complained. Clare found the newest strip of paper, Bonnie's, and shoved it into her pocket. The other two took longer to remove because they were half-buried in the tangled branches. The last one nearly disintegrated in her hand when she touched it. The strips were supposed to come loose of their own accord. Without meaning to betray anyone's trust, she read the words the crooked letters formed. "Bonnie, good-bye."

Did Mr. Younger know Bonnie's plan? No, he couldn't. Perhaps this was only his way of sending Bonnie off to California.

She shoved the strips of paper into her pocket and ran back to the front door. Instead of hanging her coat in the front hall, she hurried upstairs to the old nursery that had been turned into a bedroom for her and Bonnie years before.

She spread the wet strips out upside down on the top of her dresser. She was tempted to read Mr. Younger's again, but she did not.

Darkness fell early that afternoon, and later, when Mama came home at the end of the storm, she was greeted with the bad news about the Ornament Tree.

"It seems like the end of the world," she said. "The tree has been there all my life."

From the small parlor where Mr. Younger was enjoying — or *not* enjoying — his afternoon tea, Clare heard him banging his spoon on his cup.

"I'm not going in there," Clare said flatly. "He'll be out of sorts because of the tree and looking for someone to pick on."

"I'll go," Mama said. "He can't be worse than a library filled with wet, cranky children."

But he could be, Clare thought. He often was impossible. But he was also wonderful, witty, and amusing, caring deeply about the people in the house. And he would never guess how she felt about him.

Mama came back. "He wants to know if Mrs. Carver is home yet. And if the afternoon papers are here."

Mrs. Carver was the only woman boarding in Audra Devereaux's large house. Quiet and frail, she still volunteered several hours of every day at a women's hospital. Mr. Younger was fond of her.

"She isn't always yammering on and on about nothing," he had explained once to Clare, leaving her to wonder for a miserable week if he had meant that *she* yammered on and on about nothing.

When Mrs. Carver was home, she often read the newspaper to Mr. Younger. If she wasn't home, then he asked Clare, and sometimes, when she finished, he would ask her to play something on the piano in the front parlor. He would move out of his lair then, so that he could hear her better. She was both flattered and unnerved by this.

Disgusted to learn that Mrs. Carver was still at the hospital, Mr. Younger asked for Clare.

Winnie stopped her. "Wait one second," she said. "I'll get a bit of the whiskey the doctor prescribed for him, and you take that with you. Today's a hard day for him, with Bonnie going and the tree falling."

Clare's glance slid to her grandmother, whose delicate face was marred with a faint frown. Even before Prohibition became law, Grandmother had never allowed liquor in the house. But then Mr. Younger's doctor had decided that the blind man might feel better if he had an occasional sip of whiskey. She had protested, and rightly so, that the men boarders left the house nearly every night after dinner to have drinks at the downtown hotel where the whiskey was served in coffee cups, so Mr. Younger was already drinking more spirits than he should.

"Audra," Winnie had said at that time, "you are the dearest friend I ever had and I love you as if you were my own sister. But leave the poor man alone. He's young and blind, and he believes he has nothing left to live for. What's the harm in a drop or two of alcohol?"

"I offer you my former husband as an example of what is wrong," Mama had said stiffly, intruding on the conversation.

Clare's father had drunk his way through his own money, his wife's, and the fortunes of several investors. His time in jail had not reformed him. She shared her mother's hatred of drinking.

Winnie brought the whiskey in a small glass, and Clare carried it to the back parlor, along with the newspaper. The room was dark, so she twisted the knob that turned on the electric light.

"I brought you a dose of your medicine," she said as she set the glass with a deliberate clink on the small table next to Mr. Younger's chair. The sound would help him locate it.

He nodded and reached for the glass. "So, you ladies have decided that the bear must be pampered."

"Something like that," Clare said. She sat across from him and opened the paper. "Would you like me to start with the headlines?"

Mr. Younger tasted his whiskey, made a face, then drank it down in one gulp. "Ghastly stuff," he muttered. "Well, well, Clare. Get on with it. What new horrors are described in the news this afternoon?"

"The police are expecting trouble because New Year's Eve falls on a Saturday night this year. Do you want to hear about that?"

"Why not?" Mr. Younger said.

Clare, who read aloud very well, began. Mr. Younger interrupted her immediately.

"What do you think of Bonnie going back to Berkeley before classes take up again?" he asked.

Clare blinked. "I don't know. I guess she had things she wanted to do. Didn't she go back early last Christmas?"

"I suppose so," Mr. Younger said, sighing. "Is she going to a New Year's Eve party? The train will get her there in plenty of time."

"A party with gangsters?" Clare asked, grinning.

"Yes, or with young college devils who don't take anything — or anyone — seriously. I see no difference between them."

"She didn't say anything about a party to me," Clare said truthfully. "Do you want me to read the article?"

"What *did* she say to you?" he asked.

Clare pressed her fingers against her mouth for a moment, and then said evenly, "What did she say to *you?*"

"Don't you play that game with me, young lady," Mr. Younger said. "All right, we'll get down to it, then. Did she tell you she doesn't want to come home for every vacation? I rather suspect that she is tired of us. I suspect that she wants to be more independent. What do you say to that?"

"I don't say anything to that," Clare said, working hard to keep her voice even. "Bonnie would never get tired of spending time with her family. But she —"

25

She hesitated, appalled that she was about to tell him that Bonnie probably wanted more independence than she already had.

"She's changed, you know," Mr. Younger said.

Yes, Clare thought. The orphaned girl with the mop of blond curly hair had grown to a self-confident young woman who had made ambitious plans to enter a medical school that was hostile to the idea of women students. She had confided in Clare that the doctor with whom she and several other students boarded in Berkeley had told her she might make a better case for herself if she could demonstrate that this was not a frivolous notion. But assisting a medical missionary in China for a year!

"She hasn't changed, not really," Clare said slowly, carefully. "She always wanted to do something that had meaning. She still feels that way. You don't need to worry about her dancing with gangsters. Bonnie is determined to fulfill her dreams."

Mr. Younger smiled for a moment, but the smile vanished, replaced by sadness. "Yes, you're right about that. She is determined. But her determination will take her away from us. And we must let go of her, so that she doesn't feel obliged to keep looking back." He cleared his throat. "I, for one, will not count the days waiting for her to come home again."

Clare could only stare. She did not know what to make of his comments. Did he realize that Bonnie was not coming home in June? Or did he mean something else?

He had written, "Bonnie, good-bye." Perhaps he was letting her go. Clare did not know how to feel, and her relief was mixed with guilt.

Mrs. Carver came in then, and asked Clare if she wanted her to take over. Clare got up, anxious to leave the room and retreat to the old nursery to think over this conversation.

But Mrs. Klacker asked her to set the table for dinner, and Winnie wanted her to help pack a box of books she intended to take to the Neighborhood House the next morning. Then Mr. Malcolm Partridge, the elderly lawyer who had boarded with the family since Grandmother first turned her handsome house into a boarding house, came in shivering from the cold and wanting tea, if it wasn't too much trouble. Late afternoons at the boarding house were hectic.

Clare and Winnie were bending over the box of books in the hall when Mr. Reynolds came in. "I can smell roast beef," he said as he hung up his coat. "Good. I'm starved. Is Mr. Partridge here? Excellent. I'll join him. Ladies, if you have plans for that box, I hope they don't include moving it anywhere. It's much too heavy for you."

"We're taking it to the Neighborhood House tomorrow," Winnie said.

"My auto is outside," he said. "I'll deliver it for you first thing in the morning."

When he left the hall, Winnie whispered, "I wish you could have seen him at the station this morning. He must have shaken Bonnie's hand a dozen times and wished her well and promised to write." Winnie laughed then, and added, "Stars and bars, but we've been blind."

"What are you talking about?" Clare asked.

"Of course," Winnie went on, "Bonnie never notices things like that. So now we have two boarders languishing over her, and she has set her sights on being a doctor. Isn't life interesting sometimes?"

If only you knew how interesting, Clare thought.

What will they all think when they learn Bonnie's secret?

Dinner was ready. Audra sat at the head of her table, and the chair at the foot was always left empty in remembrance of Clare's long-dead grandfather. Mr. Younger ate alone in the small parlor. Mrs. Klacker and Mama served.

"Did you tell Winnie about the boy we saw this morning?" Mama asked Clare.

"Not yet," Clare said. "And there's even more to tell.

When I walked back, I saw him again, sitting on the curb and crying. His face was covered with blood. But when I stopped to ask him if he was all right, this awful, dirty man ran over and yelled at me to leave him alone. And the boy didn't want help, either."

"What's this? What's this?" Winnie cried.

Mama explained about the child working with the men who were repairing the street.

"It never ends, does it?" Winnie exclaimed. "Do we have a law preventing child labor? We do not. Every attempt to make child labor illegal has been struck down by that wretched Supreme Court. You may be sure that none of the Justices would allow his own children to go to work when they are mere babies. Where exactly did you see these street workers?"

Clare told her and Winnie promised that she would go by the place the next day. "If I see the child out there, I'll call the police," she promised.

"I fear they won't care," Grandmother said quietly. "I must concentrate on educating the mothers who come to the Neighborhood House. When they see how wrong it is to let their children go out to work, this will stop."

"They don't have much choice, Mrs. Devereaux," Mr. Partridge said. "Wages are so low that sometimes it takes everyone in the household to earn enough to feed the family."

"But they manage their money so poorly," Winnie said. "There isn't a woman in any of my classes who wouldn't spend ten dollars having photographs of her family taken, even though all the children will be wearing borrowed shoes for the occasion because they don't have decent ones themselves. They'll buy foolish gadgets from door-to-door salesmen, and feed their children nothing but bread and coffee for dinner. They'll spend two dollars on a new hat, when their children's teeth are rotting out."

"Education is the answer," Grandmother said.

Mr. Younger, in his lair, called out, "Dear lady, you can't educate someone who doesn't want to learn. They shouldn't have children in the first place! I think you must do more than pass out pamphlets on birth control."

Everyone at the table was embarrassed except Audra and Winnie.

"I'm almost afraid to ask what your solution might be," Winnie called out to their wrathful young boarder.

"Get the women when they're young!" Mr. Younger grumbled. "Encourage them to be like our Bonnie! And please ask Mrs. Klacker if she plans on poisoning me. I don't like cheese on my potatoes!"

He shouted the last words, so Mrs. Klacker, hearing

him, came in through the swinging door, laughing. "One scrap of cheese on his potatoes," she said to the people at the table. "One scrap! The man's like the princess in the story, the one with the pea under her mattress."

She carried a bowl of potatoes with her, and bustled into the small parlor. "Here you are, you bad boy. Here's another potato for you, and stop shouting like that, or you'll never have another piece of chocolate cake."

She was the only person in the house that he allowed to scold him. Now, mollified, he said, "I'm sorry, but you know I can't stand cheese."

"It was an accident," Mrs. Klacker said. "I got so busy grating and sprinkling that I forgot what a delicate flower you fancy yourself to be. Now your new potato is at nine o'clock on your plate, and I'll throw the poisoned one straight into the bin. Are you satisfied?"

"I want my coffee now," he said crossly.

"You shall have it," Mrs. Klacker said. She came back into the dining room, rolling her eyes. The men at the table had gone on eating throughout the conversation, finding nothing wrong with it. But the women exchanged wry glances.

"Men," Winnie murmured.

"I beg your pardon?" Mr. Reynolds asked, looking up.

Winnie shook her head wordlessly.

Audra said, "Bonnie's passing through Oregon now. I hope the food on the train is good."

"It will be delicious," Mr. Reynolds said. "But if you want phenomenal food, you must travel across the ocean on one of the fine liners."

Clare froze, holding her fork halfway to her mouth.

"I don't imagine the immigrants in steerage share your opinion," Mr. Younger called out to Mr. Reynolds.

"Carson, you are impossible," Mr. Reynolds called back cheerfully.

"I'm only keeping you on your toes," Mr. Younger responded.

Grandmother lifted her delicate eyebrows. "Gentlemen," she said mildly.

"Now, let's get back to that boy," Winnie said. "Let's make a plan."

Clare felt as if she could breathe again now that the subject of ocean liners had been abandoned.

Oh, Bonnie, she thought. I wish I could be certain that you really understand what you're doing.

3

*F*our men, under the direction of the Devereauxs'
handyman, Mr. Bascomb, cleared away the fallen
Ornament Tree early Friday morning. A dismal rain
fell steadily, melting the snow. Grandmother took pity
on the workers and sent Mrs. Klacker out to the porch
with mugs of coffee and thick slices of warm bread.

Clare, who had been watching the work from the
windows, shivered and hugged herself to keep warm.
The coal furnace seemed slower than usual heating the
big house that morning.

"It seems so strange," she murmured to herself.

"What does, dear?" her grandmother asked as she
passed on her way to the dining room.

"Not seeing the tree out there," Clare said.

Grandmother paused in the doorway. "I can't decide
if this is the end of something or the beginning," she

said. "But Mr. Bascomb said he has a cherry tree he'll move from his yard to ours, as soon as the ground warms up. It's shadowing his wife's roses, he tells me, and she wanted him to cut it down. I rather like the idea of a cherry tree holding our wishes. What do you think?"

Clare said, "It's fine, Grandmother," but she believed that a new cherry tree could not take the place of the old apple tree. She thought of the three strips of paper that had dried in her room and wondered if she should tie them to a new tree. Maybe it would be better to leave them off and interrupt Bonnie's wish. But no. Bonnie would trust her to do the right thing, even if the wish had something to do with China.

During breakfast, Mr. Reynolds offered a ride to everyone who worked downtown, to spare them waiting for the streetcar in the rain. Mrs. Carver did not plan to leave for the hospital until midmorning, so she lingered at the table with Grandmother and Winnie after the men left.

Clare's mother waited until the last minute before hurrying away to the library. "I hate going out today," she said. "But if the rain stops, Clare, I hope you'll run out to see if that poor boy is working again. He looked so pathetic."

"Oh, we'll go even if it doesn't stop raining," Winnie assured her. "If he's working on a day like this, I'll hurry downtown and see that awful Torkelson fellow in the mayor's office. He's denied more than once that there are any children on the city's work crews."

Mama left for the library, Grandmother consulted Mrs. Klacker in the kitchen about menus and household accounts, and Mrs. Carver sat down at the telephone under the stairs to call the volunteers who were planning a simple coffee party on New Year's Eve for some of the ambulatory hospital patients. Clare, left with nothing to do but drift around the big house or read, found herself at the windows again, watching the men cut and stack the wood from the old apple tree.

Burning the Ornament Tree in the kitchen stove and the fireplaces seemed wrong. But then, perhaps that was the last service the old tree could provide. Clare blinked away tears.

It was nearly eleven when the rain slackened, and Clare and Winnie set out to find the work crew that Clare and her mother had seen the day before. The men were farther down the block than they had been, still filling in the great holes in the street, but the boy was not with them.

Clare and Winnie stood uncertainly under the big black umbrella they shared. "Do you see the man who chased you off?" Winnie asked Clare. "I wouldn't mind having a few words with him."

"He's not here, either." Clare could not decide if she was glad or sorry. Winnie would be more than willing to take on a man who had been so rude to someone else.

"We could walk around a bit and see if we can find other men working on the streets," Winnie said. "But you're cold, aren't you?"

"Freezing," Clare admitted. "Maybe the boy was only out here that one time. And maybe he was hurt because he'd fallen, and not because someone had hit him."

"Maybe," Winnie said grimly. "All right, let's go home."

While they hurried back, Clare hoped that she had spoken the truth, and they had no real cause to worry. Grandmother and Winnie both knew horrible stories about children as young as five who were forced to work in hard and dangerous circumstances.

When she reached home, Clare telephoned Marietta Nelson, who had been her best friend since they were barely able to walk. Marietta reported that her mouth was sore from her visit to the dentist, but she was bored staying home and wanted company.

"Or maybe we should go downtown and have lunch,"

she added eagerly. "I couldn't eat much, but we could have tea and those darling little sandwiches at Fredericks. And we could look at"—she lowered her voice—"you know."

Clare glanced over her shoulder to make certain Grandmother could not hear. "We might," she murmured into the telephone mouthpiece. "We're nearly sixteen, and Miss Delaney said we could wear them then."

"Darcy Beauchamp's already wearing one," Marietta said.

"She's not!" Clare gasped.

"She certainly is!" Marietta said triumphantly. "I talked to her yesterday—she was in the lobby of the building where our dentist works—and she couldn't wait to whisper in my ear that she was wearing one right that very minute. And she won't be sixteen until July."

"Did your mother hear her?" Clare asked.

"No, no, but I told her when we were going down in the elevator after the dentist hurt me so much, because I thought she'd feel sorry for me and let me have one, but she took away my pocket money because I said 'brassiere' out loud. Clare, we were the only two people on the elevator, except for the woman operating it, and I was barely whispering!"

37

"I'll pay for our lunch," Clare offered quickly.

"No, I still have my Christmas money. But Mama was so angry that she says now she doesn't care that Miss Delaney changed the academy's rules about always wearing corsets and will let us wear brassieres when we're sixteen. Mama says she'll let me have one when *she* has one, and that will be when a cow flies over the moon."

The older students at Miss Delaney's Academy had worn corsets since they were twelve, and Grandmother and Mama had approved wholeheartedly, in spite of all the racket they raised about women voting, and managing their own money, and using birth control so they wouldn't have so many babies. Winnie wore brassieres, but Winnie also wore trousers when she gardened, and she had cut her hair short before anyone else did.

Bonnie wore modern undergarments now — Clare had seen them in her suitcase when she came home for Christmas — brassieres and skimpy silk "step-ins" and underslips that were more lace than fabric.

Clare ran her fingers over her sides and felt the stays in her corset through her clothing. She sighed. "I want to do something today," she told Marietta. "Anything! I'm so sick of the weather. Let's go downtown and try on brassieres!"

At that moment, Grandmother came down the steps.

Clare's fair skin burned with a blush. But Grandmother moved on toward the kitchen, and only smiled at her as she passed.

Marietta boarded the streetcar one stop after Clare did, and plopped down next to her. "Look at my hair," she complained. Her curly red hair was even curlier than usual, and sprayed out under her hat in tight spirals. "I use an umbrella and wear a hat, and I still look like a freak."

"Your hair is beautiful," Clare said. She would have traded her long, straight hair in an instant.

"We could get our hair cut today, too, you know," Marietta said. "That would show Mama a thing or two."

"You know no one would cut our hair unless our mothers were with us," Clare said.

"We could do it ourselves when we get home," Marietta said. "Beth Ellen Frank did."

"She looked like somebody peering through fringed curtains," Clare said. "Everybody at school laughed at her. And you know we can't hide short hair from Miss Delaney. Beth Ellen had to wear a scarf over her head until her hair grew out."

"Did you ever wonder what it was like to go to public school?" Marietta asked. "Those girls cut their hair.

I'll bet they wear any kind of underwear they like. Or even none at all!"

Clare blinked. "I don't believe *that*."

"And think about all the boys we'd know," Marietta prattled on.

Clare nodded. "There would be boys, yes. But Bonnie told me we're better off in a girls' school."

"I don't see why," Marietta said.

"Because the teachers in public schools only care about the boys," Clare said. "We're getting a better education at the Academy."

"But how are we supposed to meet boys?" Marietta said. "The only time we see any up close is when Miss Delaney invites them to the school for one of those awful afternoon tea dances. They stand on one side of the room gawking at us and we stand on the other side, first praying somebody will ask us to dance, and then praying nobody does so we won't be first out on the floor with everyone watching to see if we trip over our feet. And then the teachers pair us up, and I always have to dance with a boy who is shorter than I am, or who has sweaty hands and spots all over his face."

Clare burst out laughing. "There are no boys our age who are taller than we are or who don't have spots."

"My mother was married when she was my age,"

Marietta said, scowling. "She had her own house and a cook and a maid to help with the work."

"You don't want to get married!" Clare said firmly. "You haven't had a chance to have real adventures yet."

"What real adventures?" Marietta said, staring at Clare as if she were looking at a stranger. "Girls don't have adventures. We die of boredom sitting in our houses reading boring books about people who lived a hundred years ago who also died of boredom in their own houses."

Clare was helpless with laughter, until she remembered that Bonnie was about to begin an adventure of such magnitude that even thinking about it made Clare feel ill.

"We'll have adventures," she said, trying to sound as if she meant it.

"I'm going to have one today," Marietta said. "I'm going to buy a brassiere."

They didn't return from their shopping trip until the middle of the afternoon. The rain had finally stopped, and as the streetcar clattered and clanged up the first block of a steep hill, Clare saw a torn fragment of blue sky in the south.

At that moment, she saw the boy again, shuffling down an alley, followed by a small white dog with a curly tail.

"It's that boy!" she exclaimed.

"What boy?" Marietta asked.

He was lost from sight when the streetcar passed the alley. Clare explained while Marietta watched her skeptically.

"You can't be sure if it's the same boy," she said.

"He had the same kind of cap and he was wearing boots much too big for him," she said. "I'm sure it was him. But at least he wasn't working with those men fixing the street. Winnie will be glad to hear that."

"Winnie will be glad to hear that you bought a brassiere today, too," Marietta said. She handed her own sack to Clare. "Now remember, you promised to keep mine for me until I come over and get it."

"How do you think you can manage getting out of the house when you're wearing it?" Bonnie asked. "Your mother might notice that you look different."

"I'll manage," Marietta said. "I'll always put my uniform jacket on before I come downstairs in the morning."

"You won't have corset covers in the laundry."

"I'll put some in anyway," Marietta said. "And I'll

wash my brassiere in the upstairs bathroom and hang it to dry on the back of my bedroom door."

"I think I'll take the easy way out," Clare said. "I'll just wait until I'm sixteen. That's only a few weeks away."

"Coward," Marietta said, laughing.

"I admit it."

She was glad, when she walked in her house, that no one except Mrs. Klacker was there, so she had the opportunity of hiding the purchases in the bottom drawer of her dresser.

On Saturday evening, Grandmother gave her usual New Year's Eve party for the boarders. Mrs. Klacker produced a feast, and Mr. Reynolds, who worked for a steamship company, passed around boxes of exotic sweets from faraway places. Clare and Winnie made sure everyone's coffee cup was kept filled, and just before midnight, they helped Mrs. Klacker bring in a four-layer chocolate cake and an assortment of cookies and candies. Winnie filled a punch bowl with cider.

Mr. Younger was cheerful for once, and Clare thought the credit might be given to Mrs. Klacker's generous helpings of whiskey before dinner. He even ate in the dining room with the rest of them, although he usually preferred eating alone in his dark little parlor.

Mrs. Carver came home five minutes before midnight, in time to join everyone in a toast to the new year.

"And here's to the old Ornament Tree," Winnie added, raising her glass of cider.

"And to the poor souls in the hospital," Mrs. Carver said.

Clare took a deep breath and raised her glass. "And to our Bonnie," she said.

"Hear, hear!" Mr. Partridge cried.

They all drank down their cider then, and Clare saw that Mr. Younger finished first, and then held his glass against his chest with both hands, as if conferring an added blessing to the toast.

Even if he tries, he can't give her up, she thought. What will he do when she's in China?

China!

"It's very late," Mama said then. "Clare, you must go up to bed. You look exhausted."

Clare, weary and depressed, rose from the table and would have left the dining room immediately, but Mr. Reynolds got up too, took her hand in his, and kissed it. "A very happy new year to you, beautiful Clare," he said.

Clare blushed and everyone, even Grandmother, laughed.

"What's going on?" Mr. Younger demanded.

"Mr. Reynolds kissed Clare's hand," old Mr. Partridge explained. "And Clare is not like most modern young women. She actually blushed. Most refreshing."

"Ah, well," Mr. Younger said, musingly. "She must be going through a metamorphosis of some sort. The Clare I know best would have socked the gentleman in the eye and knocked him down."

Everyone laughed then, except Clare, who fled the room angrily. How dare he tease her and treat her like a child?

She felt she was not important to the household because the adults' conversation started up again immediately, before she was halfway up the stairs.

And no one, not even sharp-eyed Grandmother, noticed that she had worn a forbidden undergarment under her best party dress that evening.

4

Halfway through January, several days of warm weather surprised the people in the boarding house. Clare and her mother, always easily depressed in gloomy weather, happily foraged in the nearby park for blooming pussy willows, and filled a pottery jar with them to decorate the front hall.

Clare had nearly forgotten about the pathetic little boy with the bloody face until the third Saturday in the month, when she and Marietta chose to walk downtown to enjoy the pleasant weather. They took a shortcut, instead of following the streetcar route, and less than a mile from home, they found the boy working with a group of men who were digging up a pipe in the middle of a brick-paved side street.

"There he is!" Clare exclaimed as she grabbed

Marietta's arm. "That boy I told you about. See? He's down there with those men."

They stopped to watch while the boy pulled a sled piled with broken bricks away from the site and threw them, two by two, into the bed of a waiting truck.

"Winnie's home," Clare said. "I've got to go back and get her."

"I'm coming, too," Marietta said. "Look! That one is staring at us."

The man who had been with the boy before was watching them, leaning insolently on his shovel. He made a gesture at the boy, as if warning him to stay back by the truck, but the boy apparently had not seen him, because he staggered forward pulling the sled.

"Git back there, Jackie!" the man yelled, and the boy stopped, seemingly bewildered.

Clare made a small sound of protest when she saw the boy cringe. Marietta clutched her hand and whispered, "Let's go! There's no one else around, and I don't like the look of those men."

Clare did not argue. Together, they hurried away. But at the corner, Clare looked back. The boy had not moved. His head was bent, his shoulders hunched up around his ears.

He was awaiting a blow, she thought. And not

certain when or if it would come. She walked on, sickened.

At home, Mrs. Klacker reported that Winnie had left unexpectedly with a friend from the Neighborhood House.

"I've got to wonder what good our ladies think they're accomplishing in that place," Mrs. Klacker said.

Mr. Younger, playing chess in the front parlor with Mr. Partridge, said, "We all wonder. We can't help but think of casting pearls before swine and attempting to make silk purses out of sows' ears."

Clare could not bear to hear Winnie and Grandmother criticized, even though she often wondered why they worked so hard. "Is Mr. Partridge winning again?" she asked Mr. Younger crossly. "Is that why you're so crabby?"

"Oh, please," Mr. Partridge protested, raising a frail, knobby hand. "If only I *could* win against this man."

Clare and Marietta stood uncertainly in the doorway. "Maybe you could tell your mother about the boy," Marietta suggested.

"She's working at the library on Saturdays this month," Clare said. She bit her lip while she thought. "We'll have to go to the Neighborhood House to tell Winnie. She won't want to miss seeing him."

"Oooh, I hate that place," Marietta complained. "It's so depressing."

"You don't have to go," Clare said.

"Your mother and grandmother would kill me if I let you walk through that terrible neighborhood alone," Marietta argued.

"Grandmother and Winnie do it nearly every day!" Clare protested.

"What's all this about?" Mr. Partridge asked, looking up from the chess pieces.

Mr. Younger turned toward them and cocked his head, as if he was listening carefully, not just for what was being said, but for all of the things people were not saying. "What's going on, ladies?"

"Winnie wanted Clare to watch for a boy who's too young to be working with a road crew," Marietta volunteered before Clare had a chance to warn her with a meaningful look.

"Oh, him," Mr. Younger said. "It's all useless, my dears. Winnie may raise a storm and save one boy, but another will take his place."

"We need the Supreme Court to do the right thing!" Mr. Partridge said. He had been angry for years because the Supreme Court had declared that the child labor laws passed by Congress were unconstitutional. "You

49

young ladies stay away from the Neighborhood House. I'm certain your mothers would agree."

Any further conversation with them was hopeless, Clare knew. "Then let's go downtown," she said, and she stared hard at Marietta, hoping her friend would read her mind.

Marietta did, but so did Mr. Younger. "Wait until Miss Devereaux or your grandmother comes back," he said firmly.

"I said we're going downtown," Clare said sharply.

"And stay away from any other sort of Goblin's Market you might have on your naive minds," Mr. Younger added. Then he moved one piece and said, "Checkmate."

The girls slipped away while Mr. Partridge was protesting and laughing.

Crescent Road was nearly a mile long, a fine street lined with old trees that sheltered large houses. But it stopped abruptly at the edge of a cliff at its south end. A long dilapidated wooden staircase clung to the steep and muddy slope, and Clare never climbed or descended it without crossing her fingers.

Now, clattering down, Clare wondered at the persistence of her grandmother and Winnie, who made this trip fearlessly and hopefully. At the bottom, the staircase ended at the edge of Bernice Street, a narrow road that was never dry, even in summer. The girls hurried along Bernice, between rows of small wooden cottages that had never been painted since they had been built. The yards were bare dirt, crusted with ash heaps and dead weeds, and littered with piles of cans and broken bottles, discarded and rotting boards, and scraps of everything imaginable. Stray cats picked through garbage. Small grubby children quarreled there, throwing stones and shrieking, and a large yellow dog rushed snarling at Clare and Marietta before it was called back by a shout and a curse from a half-dressed man standing on a sagging porch, scratching his chest.

"I promised myself the last time I came here with you that I'd never do it again," Marietta said.

"I know," Clare said. "I promised myself the same thing."

"I don't understand why the boy is so important to you," Marietta complained.

Clare was silent for a moment as she picked her way through mud puddles. "It was his eyes," she said. "They were blue and round like a baby's. But they looked so old and tired. And frightened."

She did not add that remembering the shabby boy made her feel guilty because she had so much material comfort. Yes, Grandmother had financial problems.

Clare could not remember a time when her relatives had not agonized over every bill that came to the house. Grandmother was a widow who had run out of money, Winnie was unmarried and existed precariously on a small inheritance from her father, and Mama was a divorced and underpaid librarian. And Papa had never paid Mama a penny and never would, for all the ridiculous promises he had made in his annual letter at Christmas. Their fear of poverty had brought on their decision to rent out their best bedrooms. But their money troubles had never reduced them to dirt, neglect, and lawlessness.

Ahead of them was the Neighborhood House, a large, plain building doing its best to hold back the ignorance, deliberate malice, and crime around it in the scattered decrepit houses, the dark and dirty small shops, and at least three saloons that had been abandoned after Prohibition had made drinking liquor illegal and had now been taken over by several dozen homeless men and boys.

Clare and Marietta sped toward the front door of the Neighborhood House, ignoring the taunts of three small girls, who had followed them for more than a block.

Grandmother must have seen them through a window, because she opened the door. "Gracious, what are the two of you doing here? Is something wrong?"

"Winnie's here, isn't she?" Clare asked. "We saw that boy again, the one she wanted to know about."

"You came at a good time, then," Grandmother said. "She's finishing up with the hygiene class. Where did you see the child?"

Clare began telling her, but halfway through her explanation, Grandmother excused herself and opened the front door again. The small girls were still outside, shrieking.

"Now, now, darlings," Grandmother said gently, sweetly. "You mustn't run after people. Grace, you don't want to make your mother feel bad, do you? CeeCee, you and Nonnie mustn't chase and shout, either. What did I tell you? Remember? We all promised each other we'd be little ladies when we see strangers. Isn't that right?"

To Clare's astonishment, the small, dirty girls looked down at their muddy shoes and nodded soberly. "Sorry, Miss," the one named Grace mumbled. The other two wiped their noses on the backs of their hands and muttered something Clare couldn't understand.

"Run along home and help your mothers," Grandmother said, and she closed the door.

"Well, I'd like to know how you managed that miracle," Marietta said.

"With kindness," Grandmother said. "It's our most useful tool. Here's Winnie, girls."

Winnie hurried down the hall. "What are the two of you doing here?"

Clare repeated the story again, and Winnie grabbed her cape off the rack by the door. "Let's catch them in the act," she declared.

The girls ran after Winnie, who threaded her way west through the terrible slum, circling the cliff to avoid the perilous staircase, and miraculously coming out within sight of the tall downtown buildings. To Clare's amazement, they were barely four blocks from where she and Marietta had seen the wretched boy. But then, Winnie's labors for the poor had taken her through all the worst places in Seattle. She knew her way around better than any taxi driver.

Before they had walked a block, they saw the road workers in the distance.

"There's the boy," Clare said.

"I see, I see," Winnie said, and she strode forward, her black cape streaming, looking for all the world like an avenger of all the city's wrongs.

She wasted no time, but bore down on the boy, who was stacking broken bricks again. "You, there, sonny," Winnie said.

The boy looked up, pale under the dirt on his face. Winnie towered over him, and he clearly was frightened of her.

Clare stepped up. "Hello there," she said, trying to make her voice as kind and loving as Grandmother's. "Remember me?"

The boy blinked, and Clare knew he remembered her, but he shook his head.

"What's this? What's this?" The ugly man Clare thought might be the boy's father strutted up to them. "Whatchoo want with the boy?"

Winnie wasted no time on subtlety. "He's too young to be working and you know it. I'll have the law on you if you don't send him home right now."

"Whaaaat?" the man yelled. "Who are you to tell me anything!"

Another man joined them. He was slightly cleaner, and took a dog-eared notebook and the stub of a pencil out of his coat pocket. "Now then, what's the trouble here, lady?"

"Who are *you?*" Winnie demanded in turn.

"I'm the foreman of this here job, that's who," the man said. He licked the tip of a stubby pencil. "Now you tell me who you are and what your business is here."

Clare was amazed that he would speak to Winnie so contemptuously. The reaction of most people to her was quite different.

"I am Miss Devereaux, and I am head of the women's division of the Seattle Fairness in Employment Committee," Winnie said. "You know that it is not legal for you to employ a child under the age of fourteen in hard labor like this."

"Who says he's employed?" the man with the notebook said. He grinned the sly grin of a habitual bully. "Jackie's helping out his dad. It's better for him to be helping his dad on a Saturday than running around on the streets, stealing the pocketbooks from ladies like yourself who got more spare time than brains."

Marietta gasped and clapped both hands over her mouth. Clare's heart beat so hard she thought it must be audible to everyone.

Winnie stepped one pace forward, closer to the man. "I can see that you learn the same way a mule does, and so I will treat you in kind. Be advised that I will file a report against you — and don't delude yourself by thinking I won't find out who you are. By the time you finish answering questions and filling out forms, you will regret both your ignorance and your insolence."

Then she bent close to the boy. "If anyone ever hurts you — if you are ever afraid — go to the Neighborhood

House on Bay Street past Bernice Street and tell anyone there about it. They'll help you and keep you safe."

"Hey, you shut your mouth!" the other man shouted, and Clare saw with horror that he had clenched his fists.

"Pa, please," the little boy whimpered.

The man whirled and struck him so hard that he knocked him into the mud.

Winnie knelt and helped the child to his feet. The little boy pulled away from her and, to Clare's amazement, took refuge behind his abusive father.

Winnie straightened up and stepped forward again, placing herself within easy reach of the father.

"I'm certain that you've been told before what you are," she said with quiet menace. "So I won't waste my breath. But this won't go away. You may be sure of it."

She turned and stalked off, with Clare and Marietta rushing behind her, terrified. When they were out of hearing, Winnie laughed bitterly.

"Well, I know two things I didn't know before," she said. "The boy's name is Jackie, and that disgusting man is actually his father. I won't have any trouble finding him. And when he sees me again, he'll wish he hadn't."

"What are you going to do?" Clare asked as she trotted beside Winnie.

"Everything that needs to be done to give that child a life," she said. "Everything."

Clare and Marietta exchanged looks. And then, at the same time, both of them grinned.

Oh, Winnie was ferocious! And absolutely wonderful!

Winnie parted from them a few blocks farther along, and returned to the Neighborhood House. The girls, worn out with excitement and fright, took a streetcar back to the boarding house.

They found Mr. Younger sitting alone in the front parlor with a Braille book open on the table in front of him. Clare was surprised. He seldom spent any time in that room unless he was with someone else.

"Are the two of you all right?" he asked as soon as they walked through the front door.

"We're fine," Clare said, and she shook her head at Marietta, warning her against telling the curious man anything.

"I don't believe you," Mr. Younger said flatly. "I suspect you've involved yourself in something you shouldn't, like the meddling little busybodies you are. It's that boy, isn't it?"

"We didn't do anything. Winnie did," Clare said, goaded beyond endurance. "She's going to report the boy's father." She started toward the stairs, with Marietta close behind.

Mr. Younger laughed. "Well, then," he said. "That puts a different light on it. I pity any poor blockhead that our Miss Devereaux calls out to the field of honor."

Clare climbed the stairs, feeling wildly differing emotions. Mr. Younger had dismissed her own concern by calling her a busybody, while celebrating Winnie's interference.

But he had worried about her.

By the time she reached the third-floor nursery, she was smiling a little.

5

_Mr._ Bascomb and his friend planted the new tree on a quiet, gray day in the last week of January. Clare wrote Bonnie that same evening, to tell her about the event:

> _We found a tiny brass bell hanging from one of the bare branches, and Mr. Bascomb's friend told us that his niece put it there before Christmas, when she decided to decorate all the trees in his back yard. He wanted to take the bell off, but we persuaded him to leave it._
>
> _Mrs. Carver brought out another little bell and hung it on a branch. Grandmother asked her if she was making a wish, but she wouldn't tell; she only smiled. Mama says we can call this our Tree of Bells, and it will be just as good as the Ornament Tree. Mr. Younger says it makes a damned racket, but when_

*Grandmother offered to take down the bells, he said,
"Certainly not, certainly not. I can't understand
why you women make such a fuss about everything."*

*Somebody told me that people are supposed to be-
come mellow as they grow older, but that doesn't seem
to apply to him.*

After Clare finished writing her letter, she waited
until the boarders had retired to their rooms, and then
crept outside in the dark, carrying the old strips of paper from the Ornament Tree and a heavy spoon from
the kitchen. She knelt beside the Tree of Bells and
buried the papers in the soft earth.

"There," she said quietly. "This is the best I could
do." The papers would dissolve, and the wishes would
come true or not, as fate decided.

But not China for Bonnie, Clare thought as she
slipped quietly inside the house. Not China.

Bonnie answered Clare's letter about the new tree with
one directed to the entire household. "I'm sending a
small brass bell I found in Chinatown. Please hang it
on the tree for me."

Then, in a separate letter addressed only to Clare, she
wrote,

I know you've kept my secret, and I'll love you forever for that. Dr. Denney tells me that everything is falling into place. His cousin in China, Dr. Applegate, has received permission to let me stay in the mission for an entire year. A missionary, Miss Polly Edgars, will travel with me. As soon as I'm ready, I'll write Audra. Do your best to act surprised. I wish I could see you once more before I leave, but there won't be time.

Clare had read the letter alone in her room, and when she finished it, she went to the windows and looked out over the city. She could see ships at the docks in Puget Sound, and wondered if any of them was like the one that would carry Bonnie to China.

The whole thing was unbelievable. Something would happen to change Bonnie's mind. Surely there had to be another way she could convince the male medical establishment that she could be a serious physician, without traveling to the other side of the earth and sacrificing a year of her life to prove her intelligence and resolve.

She put the letter in the bottom of a desk drawer and went downstairs to listen to Winnie read Bonnie's letter about the bell to Mr. Younger.

"More racket," he grumbled as he tapped his way down the hall toward his private den. "Mrs. Klacker?

Mrs. Klacker! Can't a man have a cup of coffee in this house?"

"Yes, yes, yes!" Mrs. Klacker shouted cheerfully back from the kitchen. "Coffee, and a nice raisin bun with jam. How's that, you spoiled boy?"

Winnie laughed disrespectfully, and even Grandmother smiled.

"The two of them," she said, and she shook her head.

Clare would be sixteen on Valentine's Day, and Grandmother wanted to give her a large party at home, instead of the usual birthday luncheon downtown with her school friends. But Clare stubbornly refused. She knew Grandmother could not afford an elaborate party. She asked instead that she be allowed to take three friends to the theater instead. Her birthday fell on a Tuesday that year, a school night, so Grandmother bought tickets for the Saturday evening performance of *Blossom Time*.

On the Friday evening before her birthday, Clare read the newspaper to Mr. Younger while he sipped a whiskey, his second that day because he complained that his eyes hurt. "The Supreme Court is expected to rule that the Nineteenth Amendment is constitutional," Clare read in her quiet, precise voice.

"Oh, lord," Mr. Younger fumed. "Well, that ought to make the women in this house happy, after all the uproar they've raised about women's right to vote. But what will it prove? I ask you that in all seriousness, Clare. What will change?"

Clare looked up at him patiently. She was accustomed to that particular tirade. "Perhaps they'll elect women to office. That will change everything."

Mr. Younger pushed back his fine, light brown hair impatiently. "Marvelous. Then we'll have female scoundrels holding office. Will that satisfy you?"

Clare thought for a moment. "Actually, yes," she said. "Then perhaps it will be legal to discuss family planning."

"My god," Mr. Younger said. "Listen to you. I should think you would be embarrassed about some of your startling utterances. But no, Miss Harris. God forbid that you would have even a fraction of the tact and charm that your grandmother possesses."

"Grandmother was nearly arrested once for passing out birth control instructions in front of the mayor's office. She wasn't, but only because he had owed Grandfather a lot of money and never paid it, and she threatened to take him to court. I wish she had done it anyway because we could certainly use it. Unfortunately for all the rest of us, Grandmother thinks it's tacky to argue about money. But I don't."

Mr. Younger burst out laughing. "Oh, you beastly child. You are an endless surprise to me."

Clare grinned and looked back at the newspaper. She would have begun another article, but Winnie rushed in then, still in her cape.

"I have him!" she cried. "I have that devil right where I want him."

Both Clare and Mr. Younger turned in their chairs. "What devil?" Clare asked.

"Jackie Atherton's father!" Winnie crowed triumphantly. "Are you two the only ones here? Where is everybody?"

"Mama and Grandmother are upstairs," Clare said. "I don't know where everyone else is. Why?"

Winnie sat down. "I'd wanted to tell everyone at the same time. One of the women who comes to the Neighborhood House knows Jackie Atherton. I asked all about him, and she not only knows him, she lives across the street from him. His mother's dead. She died giving birth to her third child in less than three years. Jackie's sister died last year of diphtheria. We were right — that awful Atherton keeps Jackie out of school most of the time, and the boy works and turns his pennies over to that sot. Unless the truant officer drags him back to school."

"What are you going to do?" Clare asked as she put the newspaper down.

"Why, I'm going to talk to him tomorrow morning, first thing, before he has a chance to force the child out again," Winnie said. "I expect Audra will come."

"I'll come with you, too," Clare said.

"I'm sure the man deserves the tongue-lashing you'll give him," Mr. Younger said. "But don't you think you should leave this to the authorities?"

"Oh, bosh," Winnie said. "Are you talking about the men from the mayor's office? There's no political reward to be had from sending children to school instead of to work. The men who support politicians usually have reasons why they want babies slaving away for them. For one thing, babies don't get paid as much as adults."

"I can't talk you out of this, can I?" Mr. Younger said.

"No," Winnie and Clare said in unison.

They found Jackie Atherton the next morning. He lived in the last of a row of shacks between the mud flats and a dump. Grandmother, Winnie, and Clare picked their way daintily through the litter in the muddy path, straight to the front door. Grandmother knocked with the handle of her umbrella, and Jackie himself answered.

He was dirtier than ever, half-dressed and eating crackers. A small white dog with a brown spot on his back barked shrilly at the women until the boy gave him a cracker.

Jackie stared first at Winnie, then at Clare, and Clare saw that he recognized them. He tried to shut the door, but Winnie stepped up beside Grandmother and pushed it open.

"Is your father here?" Grandmother asked gently. "We'd like so much to talk to him."

Jackie's gaze slid to Grandmother and he blinked several times. Once again, he tried to close the door.

"Who's there?" a man bellowed in the back of the house.

Jackie pushed against his side of the door, but Winnie held it open easily.

"Please, dear," Grandmother said. "Tell your father that some ladies are here to help."

Jackie looked back over his shoulder in a panic. Someone was coming.

It was not his father. A young woman pushed the boy aside, not gently, and looked inquiringly at them with lifted eyebrows and a half-smile.

She could not have been even twenty, Clare decided.

Her dark hair was oily and mussed, and she had a purple birthmark on one cheek. She wore a soiled robe which she held closed with one ringed hand. She did not speak, but only stared and smiled in a challenging way.

"We're here to speak to the boy's father," Winnie began briskly.

"I heard," the young woman said. "He's busy. He don't like people asking him stuff about Jackie, not the truant officer or that bunch from the church. You better go."

The door began closing again.

"Jackie," Grandmother said suddenly. "If you ever need help, come to the Neighborhood House or to us. We're on Crescent Road. Ask anybody there where the Devereaux house is. The Devereaux house on Crescent Road."

But the door had slammed shut.

"Now what?" Clare asked.

Winnie glared at the closed door. "I hate giving up."

"We won't do that," Grandmother said. "We'll simply march down to the mayor's office on Monday and challenge him. And there's the school administration office. And the truant officers."

"Oh, it's not fast enough!" Winnie cried. "Anything could happen before all those...those clerks have

68

finished passing the responsibility around like a hot potato!"

Clare took Winnie's arm. "He knows where to go if things get worse," she said. But she was not sure the boy had enough courage to help himself.

While they were walking away, the door of the shack opened again, and the small dog was propelled through the air and landed in the yard, yelping. The door slammed again, and they heard Mr. Atherton yelling, "I told you and told you I don't want that damned dog in the house!"

They heard the smack that followed, the sound of a hand striking flesh.

The dog ran around the side of the shack and cowered inside an old wooden crate that appeared to have been converted to a dog house. Someone had painted "Tip" on the side.

Monday was two days away.

Mr. Younger had included himself in the birthday party that evening, so when the women in the house left to meet Clare's friends at the theater, Mr. Younger accompanied them.

The girls admired Mr. Younger. Clare often suspected

that Marietta was more than half in love with him, and there were times, especially when Mr. Younger was laughing at Marietta's foolishness, that Clare felt the sting of jealousy. But he gave her all his attention that evening, tapping beside her, sitting next to her in the theater, and helping her on and off with her velvet coat.

He leaned close to her once and whispered, "I like your cologne."

"You know it's Grandmother's," she whispered back, smiling.

"Of course I do," he said. "You have been stealing it for years. But you do it justice, too."

She could not have had a nicer birthday party, she thought.

After the theater, everyone went back to the Devereaux house to watch Clare open her gifts. The boarders had gone to bed, so the party had the front parlor to themselves.

"You won't get my gift until Tuesday, Clare," Grandmother said as she gathered up everyone's wraps.

"Nor mine," Mama said. She passed a silver basket of chocolates to Clare first. "You'll feel bad on your real birthday if you don't have something to open."

"Good," Clare said. "I like gifts." Ignoring Mama's protests, she put the whole chocolate into her mouth at once. Then she tore the pretty paper off Marietta's gift and found the piano sheet music for "All By Myself," one of Mr. Berlin's new tunes. Christiana Lundgren gave her a silver comb. Darcy Beauchamp gave her *The Mysterious Affair at Styles.*

Mr. Younger's gift was in a small box. She felt her face burn when she opened it. He had given her a silver bell, shaped like a cherry and no larger than one. When she lifted it out of its tissue wrappings, it rang softly.

"For a special wish," he said.

She closed her fingers around it and wondered what he would think if she dared wish for what she wanted most — after a miracle happened and Bonnie changed her mind about China.

She laughed, and told Mr. Younger that she would hang the bell up on her official birthday, so she would have time to decide what she wanted.

Clare's friends left, and Mama had begun gathering up wrapping paper, when they heard a sound at the front door. Winnie began to say something, but Clare said, "I think someone knocked at the door."

Grandmother looked at her watch. "It's too late for visitors."

"Well, let's see who's there," Winnie said. Clare followed her out to the hall. Winnie pulled open the door.

Outside on the porch, Jackie Atherton stood huddled inside a coat several sizes too large for him. He had the dog with him. He had used a bit of knotted rope as a leash.

"What . . ." Winnie began.

"Listen, Missus," Jackie blurted. "Listen. You said I could come here. My dog needs somebody. If you would take a boy, then you'd take a real good dog. He can keep robbers away, and . . . and . . ."

He began crying and backed away. Clare was certain that he was going to run off, so she darted out on the porch and grabbed his arm.

"Don't leave," she said. "Come inside, you and your dog, too. It's freezing out here. Winnie said we'd help you, and we will. Come in."

"I can't," the boy sobbed. "I can't. Pa won't let me. But he'll take Tip away someplace and lose him if I don't find a home for him. He's a good dog, honest, Miss. You could use a good dog."

Clare would not let go of his arm, even though he struggled against her. "Come inside and tell us all about it," she said.

He shook his head over and over, not listening, so panicked then that he was having difficulty breathing. He pushed the end of the rope in her free hand and then broke loose and ran.

The dog tried to run after him, but Clare hung onto

the rope. Jackie would come back for his dog, she was certain.

But Jackie vanished around the corner. The dog jerked and lunged against the rope, yelping. Clare picked up his bony, struggling little body and carried him inside.

"Now what are we going to do?" she asked Winnie.

6

The dog's hysterical barking woke everyone in the house. Mrs. Klacker rushed from her bedroom next to the laundry, still tying the belt on her flannel bathrobe.

"What's wrong? What's wrong?" she cried.

Mr. Partridge, Mr. Reynolds, and Mrs. Carver appeared one by one at the head of the stairs, pulling on their robes and blinking like owls. "You have a dog?" Mr. Partridge repeated several times. "You have a dog?"

"It's all right, everyone," Grandmother explained, laughing a little. "Winnie and Clare have been trying to help a boy, and he brought us his dog for safekeeping tonight. Everything will be all right."

The boarders shook their heads and went back to their rooms. Mrs. Klacker tried to pat the dog's head, and was rewarded with a sharp, warning yip. Winnie exclaimed, "Mercy!" and burst out laughing.

"Where can we put him?" Clare asked uneasily. Even though the dog had accepted her picking him up, she was not certain whether or not he would bite, and now she was afraid to put him down for fear he would take offense. He seemed to her to be quite disagreeable.

"The kitchen's still warm," Mrs. Klacker said. "Poor little thing! A boy gave him to you, you say? Let's fix him a box in the corner of the kitchen, and he'll do well enough there until you can sort this all out."

"He's probably hungry," Mr. Younger said. He reached out his hand tentatively, and Clare moved away so that he could not touch the dog.

"I'm afraid he'll bite you," she said.

"Nonsense," Mr. Younger said. "Do you know his name? Tip? Look here, Tip, old man, let's get acquainted."

He reached out again, and Clare reluctantly let him touch the dog's head. To her astonishment, the dog's tail began to wag, but he growled at the same time.

"Be careful!" Clare said.

"Oh, we're friends already," Mr. Younger said confidently. "What color is he? He feels like a dog I had when I was a boy."

"He's white, with a brown spot on his back, and some brown and black on his tail, except for the tip. That's white." Clare didn't add that the dog was dirty, and there was a patch of dried blood on one leg.

"A fox terrier," Mr. Younger said, sounding satisfied. "Mrs. Klacker, could you fix him a meal? A bit of meat, perhaps? But not too much, because I can feel his ribs, and if he's been hungry for a long time, too big a meal will make him sick."

"You know about dogs, then?" Mrs. Klacker asked.

"I know about hunger," Mr. Younger said.

There was a moment of awful silence. Clare had never asked Mr. Younger about his experiences in the Great War, when he lost his sight. With his one simple sentence, Mr. Younger had told her more than she wanted to know.

"Give Tip to me," Mrs. Klacker said. "I've got leftover roast beef." She reached for the dog, but he snapped at her.

"I'll carry him into the kitchen," Clare said.

"I'll come, too," Mr. Younger said.

"We'll all come along," Grandmother said.

"A parade," Winnie said. "No one can say that we don't give visitors a handsome welcome."

Clare said nothing more, but she wondered what they would do with the little dog, until the boy came back.

If he came back.

The next morning, Clare got up before dawn, pulled on her robe, and crept down the stairs to see the dog. She turned on lights as she went, and so when she reached the kitchen, she was startled to see the fully dressed Mr. Younger in the kitchen, sitting on the floor next to the dog, who lay curled on the blanket in his box.

"You were sitting in the dark?" she blurted.

"We don't mind it," Mr. Younger said, smiling at her.

"Sorry," she said, nearly choking on her embarrassment. "What are you doing down here?"

"I started thinking about the poor fellow, alone here and wondering what was going to happen next. So I came down to keep him company."

The dog had raised his head when Clare spoke, and now he lifted his lip and showed her a crooked row of teeth, whether in a smile or a threat she couldn't tell.

"Was he howling?" Clare asked.

"No, no," Mr. Younger said. "But I was awake."

Clare looked down with dismay at the dog. "I can't imagine what we're supposed to do with him. The boy — his name is Jackie — might come back for him. But what if he doesn't?"

"Why, we have a dog, then," Mr. Younger said.

Clare tried to imagine how Grandmother would feel about a dog running around on her precious Oriental rugs. "I don't know," she said vaguely. "I don't think Grandmother wants a dog."

Mr. Younger smiled, almost to himself. "But perhaps the dog wants us," he said.

He laid his hand on the dog's head, and the dog wagged his tail again.

They're lonely, she thought. Both of them. I'll ask Grandmother if the dog can stay.

Unless Jackie comes back.

After breakfast, Clare hung the bell Mr. Younger had given her on the new tree. The wind was weak and almost warm, hinting at spring, and for a long time she stood there, watching the morning sun glinting on the silver bell. She had intended making a wish, but she couldn't form one in her mind. She had meant to wish that Bonnie wouldn't go to China, but that would be selfish. She considered wishing that, by some miracle, the family's financial problems could disappear.

And she thought of wishing that someday Mr. Younger might look at her as he had once looked at Bonnie. But he probably would always consider her to be nothing more than an impudent child. Or worse yet, almost a relative. The Devereaux women and the boarders had become a large family over the years.

She touched the bell. The wish was almost formed in her mind, but then she shook her head.

Let everyone I love be safe, she thought instead. Let them all be happy.

The door to Mr. Younger's private parlor opened, and the little dog came out, tugging Mr. Younger behind at the end of a rope.

"Where are you going?" Clare asked, alarmed. Surely he didn't intend taking Tip for a walk.

"We're taking a trip around the yard," Mr. Younger said. He waved his white cane. "And when we are accustomed to each other, we'll take a trip around the block. Right, Tip?"

The dog plunged on, tugging against the rope, heading toward the gate. He wanted to go home, Clare knew. But Mr. Younger tugged in the opposite direction, and finally Tip turned and followed him as he made his way around the corner of the house.

Mrs. Klacker appeared in the open doorway. "They're quite a pair, aren't they?" she asked. "Your grandmother says it's all right if the dog stays, for a while at least. I've never seen Mr. Younger smile so much."

It was true. Clare longed to follow the man and his

borrowed dog, to see them together. But she went inside, instead. And she found herself smiling, too.

Winnie was not satisfied to let the matter of the boy rest until the next day when she could contact someone in city government. After lunch, she put on her cape and announced that she was returning to "that miserable hovel in the city dump" where the boy lived with his father.

"I'll have it out with that man," Winnie said. "There must be a reason why the boy brought the dog to us, and I'm afraid it's something terrible. The boy could be in serious danger."

"You can't go alone," Grandmother said.

"No, we'll have to go with you," Clare's mother said.

"Oh, for pity's sake," Mr. Younger shouted from his parlor. "We can all go, then. The whole household will march on the dump. The whole *neighborhood!* And we'll be pelted with rocks and garbage for our trouble."

"He's afraid somebody will take the dog away from him," Mama said quietly.

Winnie paused and blinked. "I believe you're right," she said. "I'll go alone. Discreetly."

"You've never been discreet in your entire life," Grandmother said. "Please, Winnie, I'm begging you to wait until tomorrow, when we might find some figure of authority somewhere to help us."

"Oh, bosh!" Winnie exclaimed. "I'm leaving right now." And she did, banging the door behind her.

She was fearless. Clare admired her more than any other woman she knew, but as she hurried to pick up her coat and follow, her mother took her arm and held her.

"No, not you," she said. "You're too young for this kind of work."

"I'm not!" Clare said. "I went with Winnie and Grandmother the other day."

"They shouldn't have involved you," Mama said.

"But I *am* involved," Clare argued.

"Wait," Grandmother said. "Please just wait. Winnie can handle herself in the most difficult situations. I've seen her. But you're not much more than a child yourself."

Clare knew Grandmother well enough to see that the situation had been decided. She bit her lip and finally nodded.

"Send the *child* in here to read the Sunday papers to me!" Mr. Younger called out from his parlor. "And where is my tea? Where is Tip's water bowl?"

"Heavens," Grandmother murmured, and she hurried off to the kitchen.

Mr. Partridge came downstairs and looked around at

the women gathered in the hall. "What's going on, ladies? Where is Miss Devereaux? I thought we were playing bridge after lunch. Mrs. Devereaux? Mrs. Harris? Isn't anyone in the mood for bridge on this nasty afternoon?"

"Mr. Reynolds will be home from the cemetery soon," Grandmother said. "He'll play in Winnie's place, I'm certain."

Mr. Reynolds had visited his wife's grave once a month for years. Everyone respected this, but Grandmother had observed once that she thought he had given up the worst of his grief, and it was about time, too. Clare had wondered if anyone but she had noticed the unusual interest Mr. Reynolds took in Bonnie's letters. But she had said nothing.

Mr. Partridge appeared to be satisfied with the substitution of Mr. Reynolds for his usual bridge partner, so he sat in the front parlor with his own copy of the Sunday paper and made himself comfortable while he waited.

Clare marched off to Mr. Younger to read to him, and try to please him. It wasn't always easy.

Mr. Reynolds returned and the usual Sunday bridge game began. Mrs. Carver came downstairs to fix herself a pot of tea, and carried it back up, telling Clare as she went that nothing was nicer on Sunday than hot tea and a good book. Mr. Younger took Tip out for another turn around the yard. The clock in the front hall ticked — and Clare watched the front walk.

At last Winnie returned.

"What happened?" Clare asked before Winnie even had the door shut.

"They're gone," Winnie said. "The Athertons have moved out. No one answered when I knocked, and so I went across the street to talk to the lady we know from the Neighborhood House, and she told me that Mr. Atherton and the boy left first thing this morning, and she thought they weren't coming back."

"What about that awful woman?" Grandmother asked from the bridge table.

"Gone, too. The house is empty." Winnie hung up her cape and took off her hat.

"He was afraid of what we might do," Grandmother said. "Oh, dear. I had hoped we could help the boy."

"What about the dog?" Clare asked.

Grandmother and Winnie exchanged glances. "Well," Grandmother said reluctantly, "I don't see what we can do except keep him."

"Mr. Younger likes him," Clare offered.

"The dog is a nice companion for him," Winnie said.

"And he's small," Mama added. "Not much of a bother."

Mr. Partridge laughed. "Oh, ladies, you'd would take in a cow if it was homeless."

Clare went to the back parlor to tell Mr. Younger the news. The dog had curled up in his lap, and Mr. Younger's hand rested on his head.

"Well, old man, it looks as if you have a new home," Mr. Younger said.

"What if the boy comes back for him?" Clare asked.

"He won't," Mr. Younger said.

But he would prove to be wrong.

On Monday, when Clare returned from school, she found another letter from her father waiting for her on the hall table. No one was around. She heard voices in the kitchen, Mrs. Klacker and Mrs. Carver planning a dessert, probably. Grandmother and Winnie would be at the Neighborhood House, and Mama would be at the library. The men all had their work downtown.

She wanted someone with her when she opened the letter. Her father's communications were often exasperating—filled with boasts and excuses. But he was her father, upon whom she had once placed her hopes of rescue from the embarrassment of living in a boarding house. He had never done anything except disappoint her.

She took her time putting away her coat and hat. Then she carried the letter upstairs to her bedroom at the top of the house. She used her silver letter opener slowly, precisely, and put it back in its place.

Then she pulled out a folded sheet and a check.

The check was for five hundred dollars.

She stared at it for a long time, and then laughed bitterly. It wouldn't be any good, of course.

The note was brief:

Dearest Clare,
Here is a little something for your sixteenth birthday.
                                        With love, Papa

Clare's hand was trembling. She put the letter and check back in the envelope, and tried to decide if she should even bother showing it to her mother and grandmother.

She went downstairs to the kitchen, hungry for company, not food. She had been right. Mrs. Carver and Mrs. Klacker were working together making a meringue. The dog lay watchfully by the back door, a large bone between his front paws.

Mrs. Klacker looked up when she came in. "You're disappointed that we're not working on a birthday cake for you, aren't you, dearie?"

"I know you'll make me one tomorrow," Clare said. "You never disappoint me. How has Tip been getting along?"

"He runs the house already," Mrs. Klacker said, smiling as she worked. "He and Mr. Younger."

"And don't you just love it?" Mrs. Carver said. "They're your children."

"Why not?" Mrs. Klacker said. "Here, taste this." She handed a spoon filled with lemon sauce to Clare. "Is it tart enough?"

"Perfect," Clare said.

The dog jumped up, pattered over to her, and surprised her by sitting up quite pertly.

"He's begging!" she exclaimed. "Isn't that cute?"

Clare held out the spoon and the dog licked up the tart sauce eagerly at first, then jumped back, shaking his head.

The women laughed. There was no doubt about it. The dog was an entertaining addition to the household.

Clare kept the letter from her father a secret until late that evening. Then, when her mother, Grandmother, and Winnie gathered together in Grandmother's bedroom, as they often did, she knocked on the door and went in.

"See what my father sent me today," she said, and she handed her mother the letter.

"Oh, that came in this morning's post," Grandmother said. "I wondered what nonsense he was up to this time."

"Five hundred dollars!" Winnie exclaimed. "I'll bet it bounces. He's not only ridiculous, he's cruel."

"But just think what we could do with it if it's real," Clare said.

"Don't get your hopes up, darling," Grandmother said.

Fathers, Clare thought. Do they know how much pain they cause?

7

On the morning of Clare's sixteenth birthday, Marietta arrived an hour before they were to leave for school. Clare heard her friend climbing up the stairs to the third floor and met her at the landing.

"You're already dressed!" Marietta exclaimed. "Are you wearing it? You promised you would."

"Can't you tell?" Clare asked as she twirled around. She felt as if her slender body had suddenly doubled in size, and was now bulging conspicuously in her neat uniform. She was not sure she had the courage to wear it to school, especially since this was also the day Miss Delaney would allow Clare to wear her hair up, or have it cut short, and that would attract attention.

"You look exactly the same as you always do," Marietta said. "You're thin as a stick, Clare. You never did have anything to put in a corset, and you certainly don't have anything to put in a brassiere."

"Thank you," Clare said bitterly. "Now I really feel terrible."

"I'm sorry!" Marietta cried. "I'm just jealous because I have to wait. And listen to me! I'm terrible! I didn't even wish you a happy birthday."

Impulsively, Clare hugged her friend. "That's all right. Now, are you ready to help me with my hair?"

"You're sure you don't want to have it cut this afternoon after school?"

"I'm not sure about anything," Clare confessed. "But until I decide for certain, I want you to roll it up like Miss Delaney's. You know, put it in a knot low down on the back of my head, so that it fits under my hat."

"But Miss Delaney doesn't have bangs," Marietta said as she followed Clare into the third floor bathroom.

"We'll slick mine back with water," Clare said. "Here, I've got all the pins Mama used before she had her hair cut. Do you think you can do it?"

Marietta made a face. "I can try. But you'll have to learn to do it yourself someday, you know. It only takes my mother five minutes to bundle all hers up into a knot. Or you could do what your grandmother does and wrap your braids around your head."

"I'm tired of braids," Clare said definitely. "Help me, Marietta."

Clare's straight brown hair hung below her waist, and Marietta ran her fingers through it tentatively. "This is a lot of hair."

"You've watched your mother, so you must know what to do," Clare said.

"Are you sure you trust me?" Marietta asked.

"It won't fall off," Clare said.

"You might wish it had, by the time I'm done," Marietta told her.

Half an hour later, the girls descended the stairs and joined the boarders in the dining room. Clare hoped that no one would notice anything different about her, because now that her hair was up, she felt conspicuous.

"My, my, look at this," Mr. Partridge said, smiling broadly. "We have a young lady among us. An old-fashioned young lady, too. I like that."

"Beautiful," Mr. Reynolds said. "You look sixteen today, you truly do."

"I love it," Mrs. Carver said, nodding in approval.

"What's going on out there?" Mr. Younger shouted from his parlor. "What has Clare done?"

"She put up her hair," Winnie called back. "She looks beautiful."

"Oh, my god," Mr. Younger grumbled. "Women. From the way all of you are carrying on, I'd have expected you to report that she was wearing a diamond ring in her nose."

For emphasis, the little dog barked once, sharply, as if he agreed with the man.

"We have a pair of devils now, back there in the parlor," Mrs. Klacker said as she came in carrying a platter of pancakes.

As if he understood, Tip barked again, and Mr. Younger laughed.

Mrs. Klacker shook her head and put the platter down. "Are you joining us, Miss Nelson? I'll put out a plate for you."

"I ate at home, thank you," Marietta said. "Do you have a dog? I thought I heard one in Mr. Younger's parlor."

"It belongs to that little boy we saw," Clare said. "He left it here with us Saturday night. He and his father seem to have moved away, so I guess we'll keep it for the time being."

"Oh, how nice," Marietta said, and she hurried into Mr. Younger's parlor. She was the only one of Clare's friends who was not half-afraid of the fierce young man.

The dog began barking hysterically, and Marietta stopped in the doorway. "Does it bite?" she asked Mr. Younger.

"I certainly hope so," the man growled. "Well, Mademoiselle, are you coming in or just standing there until you grow roots and put out branches?"

"I'm coming in, you great brute," Marietta sassed, and she disappeared from Clare's sight. "What's this? Did Mrs. Klacker give you preserved apricots and biscuits when everyone else is eating pancakes? Here, let me have a bite. Wonderful!"

"Will someone get this outrageous girl out of here?" Mr. Younger shouted. The dog barked, as if he, too, were demanding that Marietta be forcibly removed from the small room.

"Oh, mercy, I'll go. I'll get her before he turns his vicious dog on her," Mrs. Klacker said.

The boarders laughed. Mr. Younger, Marietta, and Mrs. Klacker regularly provided them with entertainment.

On the way to school, Clare told Marietta about the check she had received from her father.

"You're rich," Marietta said, marveling. "What will you do with the money?"

"We're sure the check isn't worth anything," Clare said. "He's sent Mama worthless checks. But wouldn't it be wonderful if I actually had five hundred dollars? We could pay off some of the bills and everyone could have a new winter coat."

"But wouldn't you get something for yourself more exciting than a new coat?" Marietta asked.

Clare stepped over a puddle and hurried a little to avoid a truck bearing down at them at the intersection nearest to the school. "I'd buy a drawer full of underwear like Bonnie's, and the carnelian ring we saw that day in the jewelry store window."

And I'd go to Berkeley and try to talk Bonnie out of her crazy idea, she added to herself.

"When will you know about the check?" Marietta asked.

"Grandmother's going with me to the bank this afternoon," Clare said. "But I'm not getting my hopes up."

She learned that she was right to be pessimistic. The check was deposited, and on Friday the bank informed Grandmother that the check was worthless.

Mama took the news harder than Clare. "It's amazing how many ways he has found to hurt us," she said, wiping away tears. "But I've come to believe, Clare, that he simply doesn't know any better. It's almost as if there's a whole area of thought that he doesn't recognize, and so he's blind to the harm he causes."

That night, after Clare finished her homework, she took out the letter that had accompanied the check and read it again. There was a return address on the envelope.

Her first impulse was to respond angrily to her father and ask him why he sent her a bad check. But after she had written, "Dear Father," she changed her mind. If what Mama had said was true, then perhaps he never wondered how she would feel when she found that the check was worthless.

She remembered Jackie, who had stepped behind his abusive father when he had felt threatened by Grandmother and Winnie. Even though he bore the bruises his father had given him, he still expected to be protected by him.

She did not understand, but she had the same inexplicable impulse. Her father had never done anything except let her down. Yet he was still her father. And this was her sixteenth birthday.

She picked up her pen again and wrote as she blinked away tears:

Thank you for writing to me. I had a pleasant birthday. My friends at school gave me an autograph book with all their names and best wishes in it, so that I might remember them always. I'll put your letter in the book.

> *Sincerely, your daughter Clare*

When she had addressed an envelope, she put her head down on her arms and cried.

Bonnie continued to write once a week to the whole household and almost as often to Clare. She did not mention China in her letter to the family and boarders, of course. All she wrote to Clare was that she had received a letter of acceptance from the church that sponsored the mission in China, and a guarantee of funds for a steamship ticket.

> *But the missionary who will accompany me tells me that our cabin will be one of the poorest aboard, very uncomfortable for the sixteen-day voyage. Well, this will be an adventure. Miss Edgars advises me to bring as much food as I can, because the meals we will get will not be as palatable as the ones served to the people traveling in First Class. But she told me that it would be good preparation for the food I'll get at the mission.*

Clare tore the letter into a hundred tiny bits so that no one could learn of Bonnie's plans.

Adventure. If Clare were to choose an adventure, it would not involve China. She thought for a moment, looking out her windows over Seattle.

I'd go to London, she thought. Mr. Younger often spoke of London.

Mr. Reynolds had been there, too. He had even been to China with his parents when he was a small boy. He mentioned it once at dinner, casually, not knowing that the mere word had electrified Clare.

"I was only a little fellow, but I still remember how hot it was," he had said. "And how dirty. But we stayed in the American colony in Shanghai, so we were protected from the hardships the Chinese endure. The Americans and British even had polo matches. Think of that."

"I'd really rather not think about polo, if you don't mind," Mr. Younger had grumbled from the parlor. "Polo matches. My god. What a silly hobby for a man."

Mr. Reynolds had laughed disrespectfully. He and Mr. Younger had become close friends, in spite of Mr. Younger's disposition.

Clare thought of that conversation now, and she sighed. Bonnie, why are you doing this?

At the end of February, the entire household celebrated the Supreme Court's ruling that the Nineteenth Amendment was constitutional. At last, women had the right to vote.

Mr. Younger sat at the table with them for the special dessert Mrs. Klacker prepared that evening. "Now tell me, ladies," he asked. "I'm very curious. For whom will you vote when all the city's worst scoundrels line up for the job of mayor?"

There was a moment's silence, and then Mama laughed. "You know, I don't have the slightest idea. Politicians always seem like thieves and liars to me."

"What did I tell you, gentlemen?" Mr. Younger asked. "They don't know whom they want. We don't know whom *we* want. The whole process was designed for fools."

"And what would you have instead, then?" Mrs. Klacker demanded as she filled his coffee cup again. "Your cup's full, dearie. What would you have in place of elected officials? A king and a flock of dukes? Or something like those crazy Russians have? What?"

"I ask you ladies of the household," Mr. Younger began patiently. "I ask you, please, why do you have a cook who berates and abuses us?"

"Because they can't find anybody else who'll work for pennies and hugs, like me," Mrs. Klacker said confidently as she disappeared through the swinging door into the pantry that separated the dining room from the kitchen.

Tip barked defiantly.

"Listen to that," Mr. Younger muttered. "She even offends my dog."

Everyone at the table laughed.

March came, milder than usual. Mr. Younger and Tip walked around the block together now, and Tip wore a bright red collar and leash. But often, in the evenings, the dog would sit by the front door in the dark hall, waiting for a little boy who never came.

Clare began spending Saturdays at the Neighborhood House, helping Winnie and Grandmother for two hours with the youngest children. She read to them, and taught the girls how to mend their clothes. The girls were dirty and loud, and their clothes were little better than rags, but Clare became fond of them and they knew it.

"You're a natural with those girls," Winnie declared while they walked home. "This summer, we'll give you a sewing class."

"Winnie, I can't do much more than mend and embroider bookmarks."

"You could make simple things, like aprons and skirts," Winnie said. "I'll show you how to use the sewing machine, and you'll have the girls using it in no time. You can't imagine what a step ahead it will be for them."

"Washing might be a bigger step," Clare said.

"Darling, most of them don't have running water," Grandmother said. "Washing is a challenge, even in good weather. In the winter, it's nearly impossible. But we try to encourage them to make the effort."

"Remember Melba?" Clare asked suddenly, laughing. Melba Foss, only fourteen or fifteen years old, had worked for them briefly as a cook, and in spite of Grandmother's best efforts, she had never bathed willingly. Bonnie and Clare had been both disgusted and amused by this girl who was close to them in age and a million miles away from them in every other way.

"I won't forget her," Grandmother said. "I've always felt that I failed her."

"She ran away from that home in Portland where we sent her to have her baby," Winnie said.

"I didn't know that!" Clare exclaimed.

"She did, all right," Winnie said. "Mr. Younger's mother wrote to me about it."

Mr. Younger's mother helped the poor in Portland in the same way Winnie and Grandmother did in Seattle.

And her son wished heartily, loudly, and often that none of them would waste their time.

"I wonder what happened to the baby," Clare mused.

Grandmother shook her head. "I hope she gave it up," she said. "She wouldn't have been a fit mother."

Grubby, vulgar Melba had been the source of much laughter in the third-floor bedroom Bonnie and Clare had shared. But now, Clare wondered if they had not been terribly cruel. She saw how hopeless life was for many of the children who came to the Neighborhood House.

And most of the poor children in Seattle never went anywhere near it or any other place like it. They were out there, some of them homeless and abandoned by their parents, and their lives were unimaginable to Clare.

"I wish I knew what had happened to Jackie," Clare said suddenly.

She found out halfway through April.

Winnie met Clare at the door when she returned from school one warm day when the Tree of Bells had just begun to bloom.

"You'll never guess what I heard at the Neighborhood House today," Winnie began as Clare hung up her coat.

"I'm afraid to guess," Clare said.

"Tip's owner is back. That woman who lives across the street from them told me they're back, Atherton and his son. The boy still isn't in school, and she's sure he's working somewhere."

"Doesn't she know where?" Clare asked. She was prepared to leave immediately and snatch the boy off the street, if necessary.

Winnie shook her head. "She has no idea. But I'm turning Atherton in to the truant officer, because you can be sure the boy isn't in school. That will be a start, anyway."

"We could go by the house again," Clare said slowly, thinking.

"And say what?" Winnie said. "No, at this point, we'll be ahead if we turn him over to the authorities. But I wish I knew where he's got that little boy working. I'd like to close the place down."

Clare had another thought. "If the boy's back in Seattle, maybe he'll come for the dog," she said. "He really seemed to love him."

"You're right," Winnie said. "He just might do that."

"It will be bad news for the dog, though," Clare said. "I'm sure he'll be overjoyed to see Jackie again, but they weren't taking good care of him."

"And what about Mr. Younger?" Winnie asked. "He and that dog are inseparable now."

It was true. The dog slept in his room, and was first to greet him when he came home in the afternoons from the school for the blind where he taught classes. All evening, the dog sat next to him or lay in his lap.

"Then maybe we'd better hope the boy doesn't show up here," Clare said. "For Mr. Younger's sake."

"But what about the boy?"

"I'm thinking about the boy, too," Clare said. "He worried about the dog. He would want him to have the best home possible."

Winnie did not seem convinced. "Many of the poor families have pets," she said. "I'll never know why. They abuse them and abandon them, but then they go right out and get another poor dog or cat and repeat the same miserable cycle all over again. I suppose they want something to love them, even the adults."

Clare had never forgotten the boy's sad eyes. "Everyone wants something — or someone — to love him," she said. Even her father, she thought suddenly and painfully.

Two days later, on the way to school, Marietta said, "There's a little boy following us."

Before she even turned around, Clare knew that it was Jackie.

Mr. Younger and the dog, which he now thought of as his own, were home and no doubt imagining themselves safe from disruption. But Tip would be ecstatic to see his real owner again.

"Hello, Jackie," Clare called out to the boy.

"How's my dog?" the boy asked as he drew closer. He had an ugly bruise on his face. His clothes were filthy.

Clare winced at the sight. "Tip's fine," she said. "We've been taking very good care of him. How are you?"

The boy fidgeted and looked everywhere but at Clare's face. "I been fine," he said. "I wanted to tell you that I might come for my dog pretty soon."

Clare's fingers tightened around her books. "Why didn't you just come straight to the house?" she asked.

The boy shrugged elaborately, still not looking at her. "I figured maybe I'd talk to you here," he said. "I seen you walking this way a couple of times."

"But why didn't you come to the house?" Clare persisted. "You could have visited Tip and seen how nice everything is for him."

The boy scuffed a worn shoe on the sidewalk. "I don't want to talk to them women," he said. "I only want my dog."

"You abandoned him," Marietta interrupted sternly. "Now he belongs to someone else and he has a wonderful life."

The boy's eyes immediately flooded with tears. He wiped his running nose on the back of his hand and sobbed. "But he's my dog," he said. "I only meant for you to help him for a while."

Clare put a warning hand on Marietta's arm. "Come to the house and see how nice everything is for him," she said. "And maybe my grandmother can help *you*."

The boy backed up a step. "I don't want to be stole," he said.

"What?" Clare asked.

The boy backed up another step. "I don't want to be stole by those women," he said.

He turned and ran, turning down a side street before Clare could catch him.

"He thinks your grandmother would steal him?" Marietta asked incredulously.

"I'll bet his father told him that," Clare said disgustedly. "He won't help Jackie and he won't let anyone else help him, either. We see that all the time at the Neighborhood House. Children, pets. It's all the same with some people. They want them, then they won't take care of them or they abandon them. But just let someone else try to take them in. You never heard such a racket in all your life."

Marietta stared at Clare. "You're starting to sound just like Winnie."

Clare burst out laughing. It was true. The passion that drove Winnie to work endlessly and tirelessly to improve the lives of poor people, even while she was not blind to the bad choices they made, was contagious.

Bonnie's birthday was in April. Grandmother made up a box of gifts and mailed it to her beloved cousin. Everyone in the house sent notes.

Mrs. Klacker told Clare that she had seen Mr. Reynolds leave the house with a small package with Bonnie's name on it. "I'm having a certain thought about that," Mrs. Klacker said as she rolled out biscuit dough with a flourish. "It wouldn't surprise me if he was more than a little fond of our Bonnie. Now how do you suppose the tiger in the back parlor would take to that idea, he who thinks he has the final say about everything around here?"

"Perhaps he'd be glad," Clare said, barely listening.

Next year, Bonnie would celebrate her birthday in China with strangers, and not in an American colony where the lazy rich played polo, either, but in a far-off mission with a doctor who cared for the diseased and dying.

"You shivered just then as if a goose walked over your grave," Mrs. Klacker said sympathetically. "You're not spoiling for a cold, are you?"

"It's spring fever, I think," Clare said, trying to laugh.

"Ah, *that*," Mrs. Klacker said as she wiped her hands on a spotless towel. "Heaven help the young man who's giving it to you, for his lordship won't like it."

"What are you talking about?" Clare asked.

Mrs. Klacker smiled. "Never you mind. Now go set the table, like the good young lady you are. The dawn comes later for some people."

"I have no idea what you are going on and on about," Clare said, beginning to feel embarrassed without reason.

"I know you don't, and that's charming, too," Mrs. Klacker said. "Now get out of my kitchen, dearie."

8

On the first Saturday in May, Clare helped Mr. Bascomb, the handyman, as he worked in the flowerbeds. The sky was so clear a blue that Clare's heart seemed to ache from pleasure and a strange wistfulness she could not define. The air was sweet with the scent from blooming apple trees in the neighborhood and the lilacs in the side yard. Mr. Younger sat in a wicker chair on the porch with Tip and read a Braille book while he sipped lemonade.

No one spoke, until Clare finally said, "I'll have to go in now, Mr. Bascomb. It's nearly time for me to leave for the Neighborhood House."

"Not that again!" Mr. Younger exclaimed from the porch. "Tip and I thought you would take a walk with us."

"Tip has no intention of walking with me today or any other day," Clare said as she ran up the porch steps, brushing dirt off her hands. "He tried to bite me the other evening."

"He certainly did not," Mr. Younger said calmly.

"He did. You weren't there so you don't know. He hid in wait for me in the pantry, and when I walked through, he showed his teeth."

"And handsome teeth they are, too," Mr. Younger said. "He has good reason to be proud of them." He patted the dog's head. Lifting his lip silently, the dog rolled his eyes toward Clare as she passed.

Little beast, she thought as she went through the open door. Mr. Younger would be devastated if he knew that Jackie was back in Seattle. And might come for Tip at any time. The women had not told Mr. Younger about Clare's conversation with the boy, nor about their attempts to learn if he had been put out to work again by his father.

The city's meager and overloaded social services had little or no interest in a child whose needs were not so catastrophic that he was starving. Clare had thought that since food prices had dropped so dramatically in the last few years, anyone could manage at least a simple life. Winnie explained to her that the drop in prices also meant that even more people were put out of work. There were people in the city to whom hunger was a constant companion.

"Jackie is the least of the city's worries," Winnie had said. "He has a place to sleep indoors and he has shoes."

Clare, with Winnie and Grandmother, left for the Neighborhood House shortly afterward. Mr. Younger was no longer on the porch, and Clare concluded that he had gone on his walk.

Most of the girls in Clare's small sewing group did not show up that day. They were young, and the good weather kept them away. Why should they spend an hour indoors with a stern young woman who wanted to teach them how to mend their clothes when they could play, running and shrieking, in the ash heaps and piles of trash in their neighborhood? Or charge up to strangers and demand nickels for candy?

Or steal the candy from exasperated shop owners?

Clare lavished extra attention on the two girls who did appear, praising their attempts to weave patches in the holes in their stockings instead of stitching around the holes and pulling the thread tight.

The class was nearly over when the girl she was helping looked up and said, "See what dragged himself in here!"and burst out laughing.

Clare turned, only to see Jackie disappear.

She ran after him, and caught him by the arm as he was about to run out the front door.

"I hate those girls!" Jackie said, head down.

"You surprised them, that's all," Clare said. "It's a mending class, although I'm sure you're welcome if you want to come in."

"Mending's for girls," Jackie said.

"You could learn to fix your clothes," Clare said gently, doing her best to sound as loving as Grandmother always managed to seem, no matter how awful the circumstances.

"My clothes is fine," Jackie protested, pulling away from her. "How's my dog? I might be coming for him real soon."

He had not freed himself soon enough. Clare saw that one of his eyes was infected and swollen nearly shut.

"You've hurt your eye," she said. "Have you seen a doctor?"

Jackie kept his distance and turned his face so that she couldn't see the infected eye. "I don't need doctoring, Miss. I think maybe I'll come by for my dog as soon as I fix him a doghouse. The old one broke."

Clare imagined a way in which the wooden box might break. Mr. Atherton did not want the dog back.

"Maybe we could talk about a new doghouse," Clare said. "But right now, I'd like my grandmother to look at your eye. She's very nice. You remember her, don't you? The lady with the braids?"

Jackie had backed out onto the porch now. "I've got to go," he said.

At that moment, Grace, who was Grandmother's favorite of all the small girls in that terrible neighborhood, leaped up on the porch and grabbed Jackie's arm firmly with both hands.

"I got him, Miss!" she shouted. "Hang on to him and I'll go get the old ladies."

Clare grabbed Jackie and the girl ran off, shouting, "Miz Devereaux, Miz Devereaux!"

Jackie twisted vigorously, but Clare held on to him until Winnie and Grandmother ran out to the porch. One look at the child told them everything they needed to know. Winnie picked him up bodily and carried him inside. Grandmother shut the door.

"We have to do something about his eye," Winnie told Grandmother.

"We'll take him to the hospital right now," Grandmother said. "Mrs. Eversham can watch the girls for us, and I'll dismiss the hygiene class."

Jackie protested and cried, but it was no use. Winnie was stronger than he, and every bit as stubborn. Grandmother telephoned the taxi company and ordered a taxi to take them to the hospital, and within a few minutes, Grandmother and Winnie were on their way with the terrified little boy crowded between them in the back seat.

"What are they going to do to him, Miss?" Grace asked apprehensively.

The girl's face was clean for once. She wore a baggy hand-me-down dress of such an ugly shade of brown that Clare pitied her.

"They aren't going to do anything bad to him," she told Grace. "The doctors at the hospital will fix his eye."

"His father hurt his eye," Grace volunteered. "He hit him with a piece of stove wood. I know that 'cause Billy Carmody told me and Miz Doren's Ellen all about it when we wuz watching the fire in old shed over on Billy's back lot. That's where Jackie's pa makes whiskey. The still blew up, it did."

Clare looked down at the earnest child and thought that her heart would break. What chance did Grace have? What could be done to help her in a neighborhood like this? All of them, these dirty children with their lice-infested hair and evil-smelling clothes, were as lost as if they had been abandoned in a wasteland.

"Grace, come inside and have some bread and milk with me," Clare said. "You're so thin."

"No, Miss, I'm going home," Grace said firmly. "Ma sent my sister Trudy to the store for doughnuts and a little bottle of cream for our coffee. That's my favorite of everything, big fat doughnuts and coffee with real cream instead of that canned stuff."

She ran off, her limp dress flopping, her unwashed hair swinging. Clare watched until she disappeared, and then went inside to wait for the return of the Devereaux women and Jackie.

Two hours later, the women returned, but without Jackie. He had been hospitalized.

"His eye's so infected that the doctor said he might lose it," Grandmother told Clare.

"He'll be in the hospital for a long time," Winnie said. "We thought he'd run off the minute the nurse started undressing him to put him in his bed, but he didn't."

"I can't believe what I'm saying," Grandmother said, "but after a few minutes, he almost seemed relieved to be there."

"His eye must hurt," Clare said.

"The doctor said he didn't know how the boy endured the pain," Grandmother said.

"Will they tell his father where he is?" Clare asked fearfully. The man might take his son away, just for spite.

"They must," Winnie said. "We told them where to find him, and they'll get hold of him immediately."

"But what if he takes Jackie out of the hospital?" Clare asked. "Remember Lainie?"

Lainie had been a fourteen-year-old girl who had excelled in the cooking and sewing classes. Grandmother and Winnie had had great hopes for her. She had become suddenly and violently ill, and one of the other volunteers at the Neighborhood House had taken her to the hospital, where she was diagnosed with appendicitis. Her father had tried to take her out of the hospital that same day, but the doctors refused to release the girl.

Two days later, after her surgery and while she was still in great pain, she had disappeared. No one knew what had happened to her. No one was able to find her again. Her lout of a father maintained that he knew nothing of her disappearance. Her weak and whining mother only shrugged and wept, which, in Clare's mind, constituted a betrayal as terrible as the father's.

The neighbors said the father might have sent the girl to Eastern Washington to work in a restaurant owned by his brother-in-law, to earn the money he owed the hospital for her surgery.

"We remember Lainie very well," Grandmother said bitterly. "And so did the doctor. They won't let anyone take Jackie away. On our way home, we stopped by City Hall again, and lodged a complaint against Mr. Atherton for child abuse. We'll see how far it goes."

They told Mr. Younger about Jackie when they got

home. Clare could see the mixed emotions crossing his face, his worry about the boy, and his fear of losing the dog.

"We must go to visit him," Mr. Younger said finally. "We'll bring him the sort of things boys like, puzzles and penny candy and those illustrated books about horses."

But all the time he talked, one hand stroked the little dog who slept next to him.

That evening, Mrs. Klacker brought Mr. Younger a double portion of his "medicine." When the conversation at the table turned to farm prices, which had fallen eighty-five percent below what they had been in 1919, Mr. Younger remained silent in his small, dark parlor. His lack of response was so strange that Winnie stuck her head in his door and asked him if he was all right.

The dog barked ferociously, and Mr. Younger shouted, "Good god, you are terrifying the poor beast! Why do you lunge in here shouting at us! Go back to your gossip and leave us alone."

Mrs. Klacker, scowling and sighing, brought another dose of Mr. Younger's prescribed whiskey without being asked.

On the following day, Grandmother, Winnie, Clare, and Mr. Younger went to the hospital to visit Jackie.

The boy had been bathed, and his hair had been cut.

His left eye was bandaged, and when they arrived, he seemed almost asleep. But the moment Grandmother stepped into the room, he sat up.

"How's my dog?" he cried. "I dreamed something bad happened to him!"

"He's fine," Grandmother said soothingly. She pulled a chair next to his bed and sat down. "I brought someone with me who can tell you everything about your dog. Here's Mr. Younger, who has been taking care of Tip for you."

Mr. Younger tapped his way to the bed, but before he could speak, the boy said, "How can you take care of my dog? You're blind, ain't you?"

Mr. Younger hesitated a moment, appearing to be startled by the boy's desperation. Then he said crossly, "You don't need to worry about your dog. His meals are prepared by an excellent cook. He goes in and out of the house whenever he pleases. He has a day bed in the kitchen, next to the wood stove. At night, he sleeps in my room. Are you satisfied?"

The boy's good eye blinked. "Well," he said slowly. "Maybe it's all right, then."

"Thank you very much," Mr. Younger said sarcastically.

Clare wanted to touch his arm to warn him against being so harsh on the boy. Tip, after all, did belong to him.

But Jackie didn't seem impressed with Mr. Younger's mannerisms. "How did you go blind?" he asked earnestly as he touched the bandage on his eye.

Clare held her breath. The elegant, handsome Mr. Younger usually resented questions about his condition. She expected him to lash out at the boy.

"While I was a soldier in France, a shell burst near me and knocked me out," Mr. Younger said. "When I regained consciousness in a hospital, I was blind."

"I got knocked out with a piece of stove wood," Jackie said with resignation. "But when I came to, I could see just fine, at first anyway. I guess that's because I'm not very old."

Mr. Younger's mouth twitched. "I think you're right," he said.

Jackie relaxed. "I get lots of food in here," he told them. "But I asked for crackers and jam, and I didn't get that."

"I'll bring you some tomorrow," Grandmother said.

Jackie seemed amazed. "Are you coming back?" he asked.

"Every day until the doctor says you can leave," she assured him.

Jackie thought this over. "My dad said he ain't coming back 'cuz he don't like the way they talk to him here," he offered apologetically. "But he'll wait at home for me."

"That's an excellent idea," Mr. Younger said. "He's wise to stay away from here."

Clare noticed that Mr. Younger's fist was clenched.

Mrs. Klacker began visiting Jackie the next day. She stopped at the hospital on her way to shop, and always brought him cookies. But his favorite treat remained soda crackers and jam.

The woman had a way with people that sometimes brought her information before Grandmother and Winnie could acquire it through their more formal ways. Mrs. Klacker found out from casual gossip in the halls with nurses and helpers that Mr. Atherton had never returned to the hospital. They also told her that when someone from the social services agency went around to talk to Mr. Atherton at home, the house was found to be empty again.

After she told Grandmother and Winnie that, they did not hesitate to ask Mr. Partridge for his help. The old lawyer discovered quickly enough that charges of child abuse had been brought against Atherton, but he had failed to appear at his court hearing.

"Not that much of anything would have happened to him anyway," Mr. Partridge told them sadly over coffee one evening. "It was only because he'd been charged so many times before that they were trying to get him into court to explain himself."

"What were those other charges?" Winnie asked ominously.

"They all had to do with simple neglect, dear lady," Mr. Partridge said soothingly. "The sort of thing you see every day at the Neighborhood House."

Winnie and Grandmother obviously did not believe him. That night, Clare and her mother joined the other two in Grandmother's bedroom and they voiced their doubts freely there.

"It had to be worse than simple neglect," Winnie said.

"Much worse," Mama said.

"What are we going to do?" Grandmother asked. "I know what I'd like to do."

"I don't need to ask," Winnie said. "We've got room for him here. He could have that small room next to Clare."

"Mrs. Wales can take another boy in her school," Grandmother said.

"You've already asked her?" Clare asked, laughing.

"Well, it's best to be prepared," Grandmother said.

Mrs. Wales ran a small school for young boys in her home, only three blocks from the boarding house. Many of the boys were handicapped, or so shy that they were unable to withstand the bullying and rough-housing that went on among grade school boys. Clare thought that the protected atmosphere would be perfect for Jackie.

But Winnie was not so certain. "He might be depressed if he's put with boys who've been handicapped from infantile paralysis or crippled for some other reason."

"He might be grateful that he doesn't have to worry about being hurt," Clare said.

"We can only try it," Grandmother said.

"If you can persuade the social services people to let us have temporary guardianship of the boy," Mama said.

"That should be easy," Winnie said, laughing. "By this time, they'll be willing to do anything to get rid of us."

But it took much work on the part of Mr. Partridge before the agency was persuaded. Finally, near the end of May, when Jackie was ready to be discharged from the hospital, Grandmother and Winnie presented themselves at court with Mr. Partridge and told a sympathetic judge about the boy.

They came home in triumph, waving a short document that gave them guardianship of the boy.

"As well as responsibility for the hospital bill," Mr.

Partridge reminded them. "I think your volunteering to pay it was more persuasive than anything else, at least where those dratted social workers were concerned."

"Oh, who cares, as long as we've got him," Winnie said.

Clare, who sometimes thought she was the only practical woman in the house, wondered how they would support the boy and pay for his schooling. But Mr. Partridge must have told a convincing story to the judge about finances.

They always managed to survive, she told herself. No matter what happened, the Devereaux women survived, and in style, too.

On the afternoon before Jackie was to join them, a letter came from Bonnie. Clare, who took the letter out of the mailbox on the porch post, knew from the thickness of it that it was the one she had dreaded.

Bonnie was ready to tell the family about China.

Grandmother read it first, standing in the pantry, with the silver spread out on an old folded sheet, waiting to be polished.

Clare watched her grandmother's face, saw it pale and saw her bite her lower lip.

Finally, when Grandmother finished the last page, she looked up. "You knew about this, didn't you?" she asked Clare.

Clare nodded. "Since Christmas. I wanted to tell you, but Bonnie made me promise not to. She's really going?"

"She got her travel documents the day after her eighteenth birthday," Grandmother said. "She has her ticket, everything. She says she and this missionary, Miss Edgars, will be leaving on the tenth of June."

"Maybe *you* can change her mind," Clare said. "Write to her! Tell her she can't do this."

Grandmother folded the letter and put it back in the envelope. "It wouldn't do any good. She's determined. She thinks that the only way she can get into a medical school is if she proves that she's serious. She has a good point, although it breaks my heart to admit it. Women have a terrible time being taken seriously when they want to enter one of the professions. A year working with a missionary doctor and the backing of the sponsoring church will go a long way to help her."

Clare leaned against the counter, feeling as if a great weight were crushing her.

"I'm sorry I didn't tell you, Grandmother," she said. "I couldn't break my promise to her."

"Promises are supposed to be kept, Clare," Grandmother said. "Even the ones that hurt us. Well, I'll read this letter to the household after dinner. Although I can't imagine how Mr. Reynolds will take it."

"What about Mr. Younger? He's loved Bonnie since the day she arrived."

"And he always knew she was going too far and too fast for him to keep up, poor man," Grandmother said. "He's partly responsible for Bonnie's ambitions. Remember how he encouraged her?"

Clare nodded. She also remembered how jealous she had been of Bonnie at those times.

"But lately I've thought that Mr. Reynolds has taken great notice of Bonnie. He was so young when his wife died. She was still a bride! It would be good for him to have an interest in a young woman again. And he has independent means, so he could go anywhere Bonnie needs to go."

"You've already got them married off in your mind," Clare said, relieved to find something to laugh about in the conversation.

"No, I certainly do not," Grandmother said. "Now. We must not let ourselves feel so bad about Bonnie that we forget we're about to have someone new join us here. Jackie will be coming home to us tomorrow. I believe this news will take some of the sting out of Bonnie's letter."

But when she left Grandmother in the pantry and walked away, Clare heard her sob once, hard.

Bonnie. You are breaking our hearts.

China!

9

A somber group listened to Grandmother read Bonnie's letter that evening. Head down, Clare stole a glance at Mr. Reynolds, who toyed with his spoon and never looked up from his cup.

Mr. Younger had joined them for coffee at Grandmother's request, but Clare could not see his expression. He sat next to Mrs. Carver, and her fluff of curly gray hair blocked Clare's view of his face.

Winnie and Mama already knew about Bonnie's plans. Grandmother had told them quickly in the hall, before everyone went in to dinner.

Mr. Partridge took a deep breath and shook his head. "China," he said. "I hope this doctor who advises her knows what he's doing."

"She has great faith in him," Grandmother said. "His daughter was admitted to medical school, but only after great difficulty and a wait of nearly ten years. He wants something better for Bonnie."

"I'm not familiar with the area where she'll be working," Mr. Reynolds said slowly. He cleared his throat. "Some places aren't so bad. A few of the missions are quite large."

"Her letter says the mission is staffed with one doctor who is also a minister, his wife, and two Chinese assistants," Grandmother said.

"Surely she could have found a place in this country, if she is determined to do missionary work," Mrs. Carver said. "There are hospitals on the Indian reservations, I've heard. Or she could have worked as a volunteer in one of the big city hospitals back East. My niece did that, before she entered nursing school."

"But Bonnie wants to be a doctor," Mr. Partridge said. "It will take something dramatic to get the attention of a medical school when they can get all the men they want to fill their entering classes."

"A woman who comes into the library has been to China," Mama offered. "She spent four years in Shanghai when her husband was stationed there. He was a naval officer."

"There are many American servicemen there," Mr. Reynolds said. "I remember officers coming to the house to visit my parents. We have ships on the Yangtze River, looking for pirates."

"Oh, pirates!" Mr. Younger exclaimed angrily. "That's nonsense. The Yangtze River Patrol is there for one reason, and that's to make certain the Chinese don't try again to throw out all the foreigners who are sucking their country dry."

There was a moment of silence, and then Mr. Reynolds said, "He's right. I didn't want to be the one to say it, but my friend is right. Our presence there is nothing to be proud of. The British run river gunboats, too. And several European countries have military forces there."

"Then Bonnie won't be safe," Grandmother said. Her usually pale face had turned a sickly white.

There was another silence. "They are spoiling for the next phase of their revolution," Mr. Younger said finally. "It began with the Boxer Rebellion, and the trouble has never really stopped. The Chinese want foreigners to leave. There are dozens of factions quarreling with the Kuomintang government. Bonnie could be caught in a local battle between warlords."

"No, no," Mr. Reynolds said. "It's not as bad as all that, Carson. Stop frightening everyone."

Mr. Younger tapped back to his small parlor, the dog

trotting beside him. He closed the door behind them.

Clare's heart beat so hard she thought everyone at the table could hear it.

"If that's all true —" she began.

"It's true, but China is huge and the troubles he spoke of might not come anywhere near Bonnie," Mr. Partridge said. "I've met a number of people who've gone there and enjoyed their stay enormously. Why, the parties, and the sailing and tennis and races —"

"Bonnie wouldn't care about that!" Clare cried. "She's going off to some stupid little mission where she'll wear herself out trying to help people who probably will hate her — most of the people *we* try to help end up hating us! — and all because she wants to get into a medical school! Why can't she want to be a nurse like other women?"

"Bonnie is not like other women," Mr. Reynolds said slowly, sadly. Then he sat up straighter and said, "My parents still have friends in China. I'll write to them immediately and ask them to contact their friends and tell them about Bonnie. The letter says she's going to Shanghai? That's perfect, because the Sydneys have a place there."

"She'll only be there a few days," Grandmother said, looking down at the letter again. "Then she says they

will travel up the river and then take a train to—
I can't pronounce the name of this place."

"There, see?" Mr. Partridge said. "Boats, trains. Why,
this puts a different light on everything. She's not leaving
civilization behind! There's no need to worry, friends."

But Clare read Mr. Reynolds' expression and knew
that there was much to worry about.

Grandmother asked Mr. Younger to come back in to
hear her other news, and after a moment of arguing, he
came. She called in Mrs. Klacker, too.

"I'm sure you've all been expecting this," Grandmother began. "But now I'll make it official. Tomorrow
we're bringing Jackie home from the hospital to stay
with us. He'll have the little room next to Clare's, and
next fall, after he's had a good long rest, he'll start
school with Mrs. Wales' lovely group."

"Heavens' above!" Mrs. Klacker cried. "I hung a bell
on the tree, to make sure it came about, and it did."

"Is that the racket I've been listening to?" Mr.
Younger demanded. "It sounds like a cow bell."

"It is not!" Mrs. Klacker said. "It's a fairy bell my
mother gave me when I was a child. I learned all about
wishing trees at my mother's knee."

"And other low joints, no doubt," Mr. Younger said
savagely.

Mr. Partridge stifled his laughter in his napkin. Mr. Reynolds looked up at the ceiling. Mrs. Carver and Mama exchanged horrified glances.

Grandmother lifted the silver coffeepot and said, "Does anyone else want more of this wonderful coffee? I declare I don't know how Mrs. Klacker does it. Never a bitter cup in this house since she came."

"I learned how to make coffee in those other low joints," Mrs. Klacker declared, and she left through the swinging door.

"You've hurt her feelings," Clare told Mr. Younger.

"Nonsense," he said. "A locomotive couldn't hurt that woman's feelings if it ran her down."

"Go and apologize," Clare said.

"I will not," Mr. Younger said. "Who are you to dictate to me, you sassy creature?"

"Clare," Grandmother said flatly.

"I will not let it go!" Clare said. "Haven't we had enough shock for one evening? We don't need Mr. Younger yelling at Mrs. Klacker and hurting her feelings. At a time like this, we shouldn't be mean to each other."

"In the name of all the saints, Clare!" the man shouted. "I'll apologize, if that will stop your bellowing."

He got up and made his way to the swinging door, pushed it open, and said loudly, "I apologize for my rudeness, Mrs. Klacker." Then he added in a softer voice, "I know I'm a scoundrel. You tolerate a great deal from me, Madam."

Clare thought that he sounded genuinely sorry now.

But Mr. Younger was not done. "Will you bring me a bit more of my medicine, Mrs. Klacker? All this babbling has given me a terrible headache."

"Say *please!*" Mrs. Klacker shouted from the kitchen.

"Please!" Mr. Younger shouted back. Then, under his breath, he added, "Wretched woman," and made his way back to his parlor, with the dog still following with his tail tightly curled over his back and his ears erect, ready for a fight if necessary.

The people at the table looked around at one another. "He's upset," Mrs. Carver said.

"He's sick with worry about Bonnie, and afraid he'll lose the dog once the boy moves in," Mama said.

"Life," Winnie muttered crossly. "If it's not one thing, it's six more, and all of them are annoying. Stars and bars, what a night."

"What a night, indeed," Grandmother said, sighing.

She folded Bonnie's letter and slipped it into her skirt pocket.

The following day, Saturday, Jackie arrived in a taxi, accompanied by Grandmother and Winnie. Clare watched from the front parlor window and saw the boy hesitate at the gate.

He's afraid, she thought. I'd be afraid, too.

He was wearing an eye patch and the new clothes Winnie had brought to the hospital for him. Cleaned up, with a haircut and decent clothes, he looked like a different child. Clare went to the door to welcome him.

Mr. Younger was making his way down the stairs when she walked into the front hall. But this time Tip wasn't accompanying him. The little dog tore ahead and threw himself at the front door.

"You already know, don't you?" Clare asked the dog as she let him out.

He ran to Jackie, keening and trembling, and leaped up on him.

The boy caught him and hugged him fiercely. "Oh, my boy, my good boy," he said over and over.

Clare was close to tears. Jackie couldn't see anything but the dog, and she knew that Mr. Younger was standing behind her, listening.

She turned back. He looked stricken.

"They're very happy to see each other," she said. "But you'll have lots of time with Tip. You'll see. He won't give up his place in your parlor."

"Boys and dogs belong together," he said roughly. "I believe I'll go downtown and look in at the school. Isn't there a streetcar due about now?"

Clare looked at her watch. "In ten minutes," she said.

Mr. Younger took his hat from the hall rack. "I'll run along then," he said.

Clare watched while he greeted the others on the porch, spending an extra moment or two with the boy. Then he lifted his hat to the women and made his careful way down the steps.

The dog started to follow him, but then turned back to the boy, his tail wagging furiously.

Poor Mr. Younger, Clare thought. It's hard, being second choice.

No one knows that better than I.

As she watched Mr. Younger station himself at the streetcar stop, she thought that probably she was not even a second choice for the man.

Grandmother and Clare took Jackie upstairs to show him his room. Of all the bedrooms, it was the shabbiest, but it was immaculate, and it had a pretty view overlooking the city and Puget Sound.

"I hope you like this," Grandmother told Jackie as she opened the door for him.

He walked in cautiously, as if he expected something to jump out at him. He looked around carefully, and then backed up, nearly stepping on Tip.

"I can't stay here, Miz Devereaux," he said sadly. "I might get it dirty. At home I sleep in the kitchen, so I can do that just fine. I won't be in anybody's way."

"This is your room," Grandmother said. "We arranged it just for you. See? Here's a place for the gifts people gave you when you were in the hospital. And see all the books we brought up from our library that we thought you might enjoy when your eye is better? Here's a wardrobe for the clothes we'll be getting you. And here's your little desk. Nobody's used it since Clare was your age. And you can keep Tip on your bed at night, if you like. Mrs. Klacker told me that this bedspread washes up beautifully. This is where you're supposed to stay while you're with us."

While she spoke, Jackie advanced a step back into the room again. A slow smile spread across his face. "It's the best room I ever saw."

Grandmother and Clare glanced at each other, then back at him.

"When you're ready, come downstairs for lunch," Grandmother said. "Mrs. Klacker planned something special for you."

But Clare wasn't certain Jackie heard her. He was

still looking around, smiling. It was, Clare remembered, the best room he had ever seen.

Jackie sat near the head of the table, next to Grandmother, and the dog crouched under his chair. Mr. Partridge and Mrs. Carver were there, but Mr. Reynolds had gone to see a friend who worked at the steamship company, to find out what he could about the ship that would take Bonnie to China. Mama was also absent, and Winnie had important business at the Neighborhood House, but she had said she hoped to be back in time for dessert.

Mrs. Klacker brought in the soup, beaming on Jackie as if he was more welcome than anyone else had ever been.

The table was laid the way it usually was, with a linen cloth and napkins, a service plate, and several pieces of silver at each place. When Mrs. Klacker served Jackie his soup, the boy picked up the bowl immediately and drank from it.

Grandmother opened her mouth and then shut it again. She picked up her soup spoon and dipped it into her bowl.

Jackie paid no attention. He emptied his bowl quickly and noisily, and then looked around.

"That was good," he said.

Mrs. Klacker, who had been frozen in place while she watched him drink his soup, said, "You can have more if you use a spoon like everybody else."

The boy looked around. "It takes so long," he explained.

"We have plenty of time," Mr. Partridge said as he dipped his spoon. "That's one of the nice things about having meals in this house. There's always plenty of time. And plenty of food."

All this was lost on Mrs. Klacker. "Use your spoon and I'll give you more," she advised. "That's the rule, and I make everybody mind me."

Jackie picked up the spoon immediately.

"Boys," Mrs. Klacker muttered as she served him.

Half the soup cascaded down the front of Jackie's new shirt, but he was trying.

Mr. Younger came home late, on the same streetcar with Mr. Reynolds. Clare was leaving to run up the street to visit Marietta, and she saw that they were engaged in an animated conversation.

"China," she heard.

She made her way down the steps, pausing only to

tell them where she was going, and left them behind. She did not want to hear about China.

She heard Tip bark, and looked back, to see him running down the steps to greet Mr. Younger. The man bent immediately and patted the dog. In the doorway, Jackie watched, smiling.

Maybe the problems with the dog can work out, Clare thought as she hurried up the street.

But Bonnie's going to China would never be right.

10

*M*arietta Nelson's household was different from Clare's. The house itself was as large and handsome as the Devereaux house, but only the Nelsons lived there, the businessman father, the harried and plump little wife, and the three children. Marietta, red-haired and cheerful, had a brother three years older, who was away at college in the East and spent little time at home, even in the summers. Edgar Junior had red hair like his sister, but lacked her good nature. Clare disliked him, as well as his father.

Marietta had a younger sister, only nine years old, and she was the reason for Clare's visit that day. Sarah had pale blond hair and light blue eyes that were as sad as Jackie's. For a reason Clare could not understand, her father treated her as if she was the family scapegoat. He never wasted an opportunity to ridicule the child, and while he was not an especially good father to his other children, his treatment of Sarah was cruel. Sarah lacked Marietta's resilience. She was so shy that visitors to the house seldom saw her. She walked alone to Miss Delaney's Academy for Young Women, keeping a careful block behind Marietta and Clare. She seemed to have no friends.

Clare entered the Nelson house through the side door, as usual. Mrs. Nelson was in the dining room, conferring with the downstairs maid, and she smiled briefly at Clare when she walked in. "Marietta's upstairs, fussing with her hair," she said.

"Is Sarah home?" Clare asked.

Mrs. Nelson looked startled. "Of course, dear. What do you want with her?"

"Did Mama or Grandmother tell you about Jackie? He's moved in now, and I think it would be nice if Sarah met him. They're almost the same age, and Jackie's lonely and not very well. I know he'd be glad if he had a visitor."

Mrs. Nelson pressed one finger against her lips as she considered his. "Well, dear, I don't know how Papa would feel about this. Your grandmother did mention the boy to us, but he's not — I'm sure you understand — he's not *quite* the sort of companion we'd like for our Sarah."

Clare longed to shout that no one was suggesting that a marriage contract between the two children be prepared. But instead, she said, "You can be sure that they would be chaperoned, Mrs. Nelson. You know how strict Grandmother is about behavior."

The maid, a young woman with freckles, struggled with a smile and hid it by turning her head. Even the servants in the neighborhood knew that Audra Devereaux had impeccable manners and a respected social position. But she was also an avid worker for women's rights. Mrs. Nelson, who left a finishing school at fifteen to marry her father's younger partner, not only did not support women's rights but barely understood them. Clare suspected that her grandmother actually frightened Mrs. Nelson.

She made the most of that thought. "Many people are interested in Grandmother's work with the poor," she said. "Only last month she spoke at the Capital Women's Club, raising funds for the Neighborhood House, and now she has been invited by the mayor's wife to become a member."

Mrs. Nelson wanted nothing more in the world than an invitation to join the Capital Women's Club. Clare knew that, but did not bother to add that her grandmother had laughed while she wrote a lovely refusal to the formal invitation.

"The boy who is living with you is how old?" Mrs. Nelson asked. Clare could see that she was changing her mind.

"Eight, almost nine," Clare said. "He's very small for his age. And you know he's been terribly ill. It would be wonderful if Sarah could come to visit, and perhaps read to him for a while. We took turns reading to him when he was in the hospital, and he enjoys it so much."

"He can't read?" Mrs. Nelson asked.

"He can, but he nearly lost his sight in one eye, and so he must not even try to read for many weeks yet. This summer he'll be tutored by someone, and then he'll go to Mrs. Wales' school."

"Mrs. Wales' school." Mrs. Nelson brightened, glanced sideways at the maid to see if she could catch her showing an interest in the conversation, and finally said, "Well, I suppose it can't hurt. Not for a few minutes now and then, anyway."

"Then may I tell Sarah about it?" Clare asked.

"You may," Mrs. Nelson said. "But I'm not certain you can persuade her to do it. She's stubborn, you know. A very stubborn and sullen child."

Clare hurried out into the hall and nearly collided with Marietta, who was grinning widely.

"Aren't you clever?" Marietta whispered. "You're getting to be as good as your grandmother at persuading people to do what they don't want to do."

"I wish I were!" Clare said heartily. "Where's Sarah? Let's see if I can persuade her."

"She's playing with her dolls in my dressing room," Marietta said. "She's turned the place into a little house for them."

They found the child there, brushing a doll's long hair. Doll furniture had been set around on the dressing room floor, and a tea party had been arranged in one corner with small china cups and saucers set on a doll-sized wicker table.

Sarah looked up when Clare entered but said nothing.

"Did you hear about the boy who's come to live with us?" Clare asked her.

Sarah tied a ribbon in the doll's hair and sat her on a little bench. "I heard about him," she said.

"He just got out of the hospital this morning," she said. "Would you like to come and see him someday, when he's feeling a little better and when you've had a chance to think about it and make some plans?"

Sarah fluffed the doll's skirt. "Maybe," she whispered.

"You could tell me when you're ready," Clare said. "Some morning on our way to school, you could mention that you'd like to visit Jackie for a minute or two. He's got a very nice little dog."

"I've seen that dog," the girl said. She picked up

another doll and adjusted its petticoats. "I've seen him walking with Mr. Younger. He barks."

"I know," Clare agreed. "But Mr. Younger wouldn't let him hurt you. And neither would Jackie."

Sarah's mouth worked, as if she might say something, but then she turned her back and busied herself with the tea set. "Good-bye," she whispered.

Clare and Marietta left her to her little world in the dressing room.

"She breaks my heart," Marietta told Clare after they went into the upstairs parlor and closed the door. "I don't know why Mama can't see that Pa has to stop picking on Sarah. She tries to be perfect, but nothing she does suits him. She cries herself to sleep nearly every night."

"Your father picks on you, too," Clare said sympathetically.

"Yes, but I have Grandma McDougal's red hair and temper," Marietta said. "Pa doesn't get much satisfaction from picking on me. Or on Eddie, either. But Sarah is shy, so it's easy to hurt her."

The girls picked through a silver dish of chocolates, selected their favorites, and sat down together.

"I have more news," Clare said. "You won't believe this. Bonnie's going to China."

"China!" exclaimed Marietta. "Why would she do something like that?"

Clare explained, and Marietta listened, shaking her head the whole time. "I wish I had half her courage," she said. "If I did, I'd go to New York. I was looking through some of Mama's old magazines last night, and I read an article about New York. I'd like to go there and get a job, maybe on a newspaper. Or a magazine!"

"Last month you told me you wanted to get a job downtown in one of the department stores as soon as you graduate from Miss Delaney's," Clare said. "You'd better make up your mind. We graduate next year. Probably you ought to go to college if you want to work on a newspaper."

Marietta leaped up to get two more chocolates, gave one to Clare, and said, "I'm not like you, Clare. I'm not anything like the women in your house. I can't imagine what Pa would say if I asked him to let me to go college. I know he wouldn't do it, so there's no point in hoping. Anyway, I will have had enough of school when I finish high school. I want a life!"

Clare took a small bite of her chocolate. "Your parents would let you go to New York?" she asked.

"No, but I'd just go," Marietta said. "How could they stop me, if I found enough money? I've got what Grandma McDougal left me, but Pa has control of it until I'm twenty-five. That's not fair, but that's how it is. But if

I could talk Mama into letting me have money without telling Pa, then I could go."

"How could she get the money without his knowing?" Clare asked. Marietta had told her more than once that her father was stingy.

"Mama's got cash hidden away that Pa doesn't know anything about," Marietta said. "She told me once that all girls should have 'door slamming' money."

"What's 'door slamming' money?" Clare asked.

"It's enough money to run away if you have to," Marietta said. "Her mother told her that she should save a little bit out of each week's food money and hide it, so that if something awful happens she'd have enough to run away."

"What are you talking about?" Clare asked, mystified.

"If her husband beats her," Marietta said.

Clare stared at her. "If I had a husband and he beat me, I'd hit him back. I wouldn't need 'door slamming' money."

Marietta looked at her with sympathy. "Clare, you don't know the first thing about married people."

"I certainly do!" Clare said. "My parents were married."

"But your father left your mother when you were only a baby. And when he came back to see you, you hated him. Just think how awful things would have been if he had stayed and your mother had to run away to save herself or you?"

Clare thought about this for a long moment, and then said, "Mama had Grandmother for a mother. I don't think either of them runs away from anything. But Mrs. Carver — you know her — she had a terrible husband who locked her up in a mental institution so he could steal the money she inherited from her father. She could have used 'door slamming' money."

"Every woman needs it," Marietta said. "But Mama's not using hers, and I wish she'd let me have it next year. Then I'd go to New York. You just bet I would."

Clare went home soon afterward, uncomfortable with the conversation and wondering why she had not suspected that Marietta had the capacity to run away. Bonnie was soon to leave for China, and when she returned, she would go to medical school.

But what do I want? Clare thought as she climbed the steps to her own porch. What do *I* want?

She opened the door and smelled bread baking. Mr. Partridge and Winnie were sharing a newspaper in the front parlor and only glanced up, smiling, at her. Grandmother was dusting books in the library, humming under her breath. Mrs. Carver was showing Jackie how to build a house of cards on the dining room table. The dog napped under his chair.

"How are you feeling, Jackie?" Clare asked.

"I'm very busy," he said, dismissing her as he frowned with concentration.

"Clare, come in and read the paper to me," Mr. Younger called out from his parlor. "Please," he added.

Clare returned to the front hall and took one of the afternoon papers from the table. On her way through the dining room, she said, "Jackie, may I borrow Tip for a while? I think Mr. Younger might like company while I read to him."

"If he wants to go, it's all right," Jackie said, intent on placing a card on top of the precarious pile.

"Come on, Tip," Clare called from the door to the back parlor. "Here, Tip."

The dog merely looked at her.

"You call him," she told Mr. Younger, who was sitting in his usual chair, drinking tea.

Mr. Younger snapped his fingers and said, "Tip."

The dog scrambled out from under the chair and ran to Mr. Younger, nearly upsetting his tea as he jumped into his lap.

This will work out, Clare thought. I know it will.

And this is what I want. Wouldn't Bonnie laugh if she knew that I didn't want a career or travel? Wouldn't she laugh if she knew I liked to be home, watching things turn out right, even if they're only small things?

She sat in the light from the window and unfolded the paper. "Shall I start with the headlines on the first page, or go straight to the theater section?" she asked. "I know you like that best."

"What color dress are you wearing?" Mr. Younger asked.

Clare stared at him. His face was turned toward her expectantly.

"It's white," she said. "Why?"

He hesitated a moment and then said, "I like to know what people are wearing," he said. "You smell very nice, too. Is it polite to mention something like that?"

"I don't think so," Clare said slowly. "Grandmother would say that was too personal."

"Nevertheless," Mr. Younger said. "You smell quite nice. Like lilacs."

Clare laughed. "Marietta and I were experimenting with her mother's cologne," she confessed.

"Ah," he said, nodding. "Begin with the headlines, please, unless they have something to do with politics. I don't think I can tolerate politics on a day like this, with a new friend in the house and a young lady who smells like spring flowers."

Clare gawked at him in amazement. "How much of your medicine have you had today?" she blurted.

He laughed. "Not a drop, Miss Know-It-All. Not a single drop."

Clare looked down at the paper. The first headline she saw contained the word *China*, so she went past it. "Here's something about radio stations," she said.

"Oh, read that!" Mr. Younger said enthusiastically. "I've been considering getting a wireless radio."

Clare laughed. "You'd better ask Grandmother first," she said. "She had trouble accepting the telephone and the gas stove in the kitchen. I can't imagine what she'd think about a radio."

That evening at dinner, Mr. Reynolds told them that he had written his parents and expected that they would inform their friends in Shanghai about Bonnie's arrival there on June 26.

"I talked to my friend in the passenger office at the steamship company, too," he said. "He says the ship Bonnie will be sailing on is old but quite adequate. However, he suggests that she try to find better accommodations aboard. There is still time for her to arrange for a cabin in Second Class at least, if she can't manage First Class."

Grandmother looked thoughtful. "Bonnie can afford

it, but I doubt if her traveling companion can. But Bonnie is generous."

"Second Class is nearly as nice," Mr. Reynolds said. "They would have much better food. And if money is a problem..." He let the sentence go unfinished.

Grandmother frowned faintly. "Bonnie has no financial concerns," she said quietly, firmly. "Her inheritance provides for her. I have already written to her, explaining that she does not need the adventure of traveling in a cramped cabin below deck. Her companion has suffered through something like that, apparently. She can tell Bonnie all about this grand adventure while they are relaxing over their tea in more comfortable circumstances."

Mr. Reynolds and Mr. Partridge laughed. Mama smiled at Clare and said, "Your grandmother has a tidy way of explaining things, doesn't she?"

"I didn't know you were writing to Bonnie, Audra," Winnie said. "I wrote her, too, and told her to insist on an outside cabin and a well-placed deck chair. Poverty is not an adventure, and I don't like seeing young girls pretending that it is and then learning the hard way that comfort is not something to be scorned."

Clare had been plagued with envy and confusion when she first learned of Bonnie's plans. But now, for the first time, she looked around the table and felt content.

I like this, she thought. I like knowing that every evening we'll all be here talking, and nothing much will change. Not for us, anyway.

"Bonnie will probably be seasick the whole time," Mr. Younger shouted from his parlor. "And it will serve her right. Jackie, come in here with Tip and sit with me a while. Mrs. Klacker promised that she would give me crackers and jam, too. I want to see what this magical dessert of yours is like."

Jackie, who had been half asleep while his elders droned on and on about someone named Bonnie, slid off his chair, called his dog, and joined Mr. Younger.

"I hate the dark," Clare heard him tell Mr. Younger. "Why don't you turn on the lamp? I can only see with one eye, but I got to have light to do it."

"Stop complaining and sit down," Mr. Younger said. "What a racket! What would you think if I told you I'm going to buy a wireless radio?"

"What's a wireless radio?" Jackie asked.

Clare glanced at Grandmother and saw her roll her eyes. "Heavens," Grandmother murmured. "What next?"

I love this place, Clare thought. With all our troubles, and people leaving and arriving, this is where I want to be.

Now, how do I tell Mama and Grandmother—and Winnie!—something as boring as that?

Late in the evening, after Jackie had been settled in bed and the boarders had retired, Clare slipped downstairs barefoot, in her robe, to heat milk for herself on the gas stove in the kitchen. She would not be able to sleep well that night. Too much had happened during the day. And then there was Bonnie — and China.

She turned on the hall light, and as she passed the dining room door, she looked through the dark room and saw that the light was on in the small side parlor. Mr. Younger must have forgotten to turn it off when Jackie went upstairs.

Mr. Younger was still there. The moment she entered the room, he looked up.

"Clare?" he asked.

"You're still here?" she said. "I thought you'd gone upstairs when Mr. Partridge did. Your light's on. Do you want me to turn it off?"

"No, no, I'll take care of it," he said. "Why are you up at this hour?"

"I want hot milk," she said. "Shall I fix you some, too?"

"I hate hot milk," he said. "It reminds me of nursery days and having measles."

Clare grinned and was glad he couldn't see her expression. "I can't imagine you with measles."

"What are you wearing?" the man asked.

"None of your business," Clare said. "I'm going to the kitchen now. Good night."

"Good night," he said pleasantly. She thought she heard laughter in his voice.

11

Dear Clare,

I received letters from Audra and Winnie, but before I had a chance to answer them, your note came, telling me that they had taken my news better than I had hoped. I think they see the sense in my plans. I'm glad, too, that Mr. Younger was no crankier than usual. After all, it was he who put me on this path. Jackie sounds as if he is a wonderful addition to the family. You have a way with children. Give my love to everyone and please forgive me for this brief letter. I'm leaving soon and I have final examinations this week.

Love, Bonnie

Clare answered the note, although she was not certain Bonnie would receive it before she left for China. She still found the whole idea of Bonnie's working halfway around the world for a year to be unbelievable. Yet, Bonnie was going.

Jackie's eye patch was removed the first week of June. His eye appeared normal, but Clare thought that he still did not see well. When Grandmother asked the boy to bring the sugar bowl from the sideboard, the boy clearly could not see the bowl until he was nearly touching it. There were times when he called Tip in a panicked voice, almost as if he thought the dog had disappeared, and startled the animal out of a nap only ten feet away.

She mentioned her concerns to Grandmother and Winnie, who had observed the same thing. Jackie was taken back to one of the doctors, who, Grandmother reported, was astonished that they had not been told that Jackie was extremely nearsighted, and the condition had nothing to do with the injury.

"Jackie will need glasses," Grandmother said. "But not quite yet. They want to wait until they are certain his injured eye has recovered as much as it can."

Jackie, listening to this conversation, said worriedly, "I don't need glasses. Pa says glasses are for sissies."

No matter how Grandmother and Clare explained, Jackie was adamant. Finally he ran off to the kitchen with Tip, and left Clare and Grandmother to shake their heads.

Sarah, shy and hesitant, came on the first Saturday in June, bringing with her a favorite book.

Clare introduced Jackie to her in the front parlor, explaining to Jackie that Sarah wanted to read to him.

"I can read my own self," Jackie said, clearly embarrassed.

"But not until your eyes are better," Clare reminded him.

"But I don't want a girl to read to me," Jackie said.

Mr. Younger had come in the front door and overheard the conversation. "Jackie," he said. "Mind your manners."

Sarah, already trembling, withdrew behind Clare.

"You're frightening Jackie and Sarah," Clare told Mr. Younger.

He hung up his hat and turned to face the children. "Did I frighten you, Jackie?"

Jackie, astonished, said, "No."

"And Sarah, do I frighten you?" Mr. Younger asked.

Appalled at the attention, Sarah whispered, "I don't think so."

"Very good," Mr. Younger declared. "Now, let us prevail upon Mrs. Klacker for something to eat, and then Sarah can read to Jackie in the library while Clare reads to me in the back parlor."

He strolled off and Jackie followed, imitating his walk and the swing of his shoulders. Sarah looked up at Clare for guidance.

"They're going to have a snack," Clare said. "Would you like something, too?"

Sarah shook her head wordlessly.

"Then let's wait in the library until Jackie is finished," she said. "It's very nice in there, and Grandmother has a book about dolls. Would you like to look at it?"

Sarah nodded and Clare took her into the small room where bookcases rose from floor to ceiling. Sarah sat in a large leather chair, and Clare handed her the book.

"How is your family?" Clare asked.

"Fine, thank you," Sarah said. And then she surprised Clare by asking, "Is Bonnie really going to that place where everybody eats poisoned poppies until they die?"

Clare stared, and then understood what Sarah meant. It was obvious that her mother had been talking about Bonnie's coming adventure in China, where opium addiction was common.

"Bonnie's going to work with a missionary doctor," she said.

"Taking care of people who have been poisoned?" Sarah asked anxiously.

"No," Clare said. "Just regular people like us."

Jackie came in then, wiping his face furiously with his sleeve. "Mrs. Klacker just about rubs the skin off me with that old soapy rag," he complained.

Sarah gawked at him.

"I'll leave you two by yourselves," Clare said. "Sarah, I'm sure Grandmother wouldn't mind if you took the doll book home to read."

Sarah's grateful smile lit up the room.

Jackie and his dog sat on the sofa, and Sarah opened *Hans Brinker, or the Silver Skates,* and began reading on the first page in her soft voice.

Clare closed the sliding door gently.

She joined Mr. Younger in his parlor, but before she sat down, he said, "What are you wearing today?"

"A white shirt and a light blue skirt," she said. "Now. Shall I read to you from the new magazines, or shall we pick up where we left off with *Kristin Lavransdatter?*

"How can you be so calm, when Bonnie is leaving one week from today?" he asked.

"How can *you?*" she responded without looking at him.

He sighed. "It's difficult, because I feel responsible."

"Because you encouraged her?" Clare asked. "Bonnie would have found her own way."

"And what about you?"

Clare looked up and found him facing her, the light reflecting off his dark glasses. "What about me?"

"What exotic plans do you have?" he asked. "A career in music? You play very well. Or perhaps you want to teach at that school you adore? The University of Washington can accommodate you quite nicely in those plans."

He doesn't want me to reach as far as Bonnie has, she thought. But she didn't share his opinions about how she should spend her life.

"I haven't decided anything yet," she said.

"What about your friend?"

She was tempted to tell him that Marietta wanted to live in New York. Instead, she said, "She hasn't decided anything, either."

"Both of you will be whisked away by young men," Mr. Younger said.

She glanced up at him quickly, expecting to see his usual wry expression. But instead, he actually looked interested. Clare was so uncomfortable with the conversation that she came close to putting down the book and leaving the room.

He sensed her discomfort. "Read now, please," he said. "I've intruded enough on your privacy."

She read gratefully.

What a strange man. But he was so dear in spite of it.

Bonnie wrote quick notes twice more before she left, the second coming on Saturday, when they knew she was already at sea.

I love you all. I'll send you diary letters to keep you informed of everything we see and do.

The day might have been depressing beyond bearing, if Jackie had not distracted them, first by bringing in an injured bird he had found in the street, and then by enraging the streetcar conductor when he lined up rocks on the tracks and sat down on the curb to watch for the results. The bird died, unfortunately, and the conductor's shouts attracted the attention of most of the neighborhood.

"You young thug!" the man yelled. "Are you trying to derail the car?"

Jackie, with Tip close behind, disappeared around the back of the house, and left Winnie to defend him while the conductor kicked the rocks off the tracks.

Winnie and Clare caught Jackie in the back yard, hiding behind the hedge. "What possessed you to do something that destructive?" Winnie demanded.

"All the boys do it," Jackie said. But his face was red

and his lower lip shook. "Nobody will get hurt as long as you don't do it on a hill."

"Don't you have something nice to do?" Winnie cried.

Jackie ran inside, weeping. Winnie would have followed, but Clare touched her arm.

"He feels terrible about the bird," she said. "I think he was trying to distract himself."

"By killing a dozen people on a streetcar?" Winnie asked. But then she sighed. "You understand him better than anyone else here, except for Mr. Younger. Come along with Audra and me to the Neighborhood House, and work some of your magic there. Would you like to start a new sewing class for the summer?"

"You said I could learn to use a sewing machine and then teach the girls," Clare said. "And I'd like to learn to cook. Couldn't I join one of the cooking classes?"

"At Neighborhood House?" Winnie exclaimed. "Certainly not. Whatever gave you an idea like that? Anyway, you don't need to cook. Your talents are needed elsewhere."

"What talents?" Clare asked. "I don't have any."

"You are an accomplished musician," Winnie said. "You show a great gift for working with children. Those things can be developed in college. Meanwhile, if you want to show the girls some simple sewing, that would be fine."

"I want to learn something practical, more than how to mend socks," Clare said. "I want to know how to run a house so that I can show the girls."

Winnie blinked. "Why would you want to do that? We have Mrs. Klacker. You help out, along with the rest of us, with the dusting and making beds. But you are meant for other things. Look at Bonnie. She's putting her intelligence to good use."

Clare could not argue the point. It was obvious that intelligent women should do things that used their abilities. But what was so wrong with learning how to manage one's own house? The women in the boarding house had once or twice been left to do the cooking themselves, with disastrous results. Was learning how to prepare a good meal so degrading?

It seemed to Clare that there was something wrong with the ideas about women's independence if they did not include the women being able to care for themselves in all ways. When she was younger, she had felt differently, but now she saw that true independence comes when someone has charge of all aspects of her own life.

What if she not only learned how to cook, but also to make her own clothes? And raise vegetables? And even preserve them? Then would she not have truly useful things to teach the girls in the Neighborhood House?

Mrs. Klacker interrupted their discussion by coming out to tell them that Jackie was weeping hysterically because she had buried the dead bird without giving it a funeral, and he was insisting that someone dig the bird back up so that the rites could be performed.

"And Sarah is at the door, wanting to know if she should read to Jackie now," Mrs. Klacker added.

"Where did you bury the bird?" Clare asked.

Mrs. Klacker pointed to the flowerbed by the back porch.

Clare sighed. "I'll think of something," she said. "Perhaps a memorial service. Even Sarah might like that."

"Mercy," Mrs. Klacker muttered, and she went back inside.

Winnie looked at her watch. "This is a long day," she said.

"You're thinking about Bonnie, aren't you? Starting off on her big adventure."

"There are adventures waiting for you, too, Clare," Winnie said.

But Clare did not reply. She went inside, to find Jackie and Sarah, and plan a memorial service for the bird.

Bonnie's first letter, in the form of a diary entry, came ten days later, mailed from Hawaii.

You have never seen anything like this place. The beaches are incredibly beautiful, and there is a fine hotel here, overlooking the sand and the water. We stayed only a few hours in the town, and then returned to the ship, but I have promised myself that one day I will spend more time in this paradise.

The next letter came near the end of June, mailed from the Philippine Islands. They knew that Bonnie was in China by that time, but the letter spoke only of a storm at sea and pleasant dinner companions and shuffleboard on deck.

Mr. Coleman, who plays shuffleboard with us, lives in Shanghai, and he promises to show me the sights before I leave on the river journey to Nanking. His father teaches at the university there, and both of his sisters are engaged to American Naval officers. He says there are more than sixty thousand Westerners in Shanghai alone, and they have wonderful times. But Miss Edgar says they are not our sort, being, for the most part, decadent and idle. She dislikes Mr. Coleman, and prays for him every night. Aloud. I think she means for me to hear the prayers and re-form myself before it is too late!

Most of the people at the dinner table laughed at this. Mr. Partridge said, "Our Bonnie is irrepressible, isn't she?"

But Clare saw that Mr. Reynolds only stirred extra sugar into his coffee.

Jackie, bored with the letter from this Bonnie whom he had never met, fiddled with his milk glass until he succeeded in spilling it, and then incurred Mrs. Klacker's wrath by giving Tip a cracker with jam on it, which the dog promptly dropped jam-side-down on the carpet.

"When are you going to learn manners?" she demanded as she cleaned up the mess.

"Maybe I'll go eat with Mr. Younger," the boy said. "He can't see so he won't care if I spill."

"A sound idea!" Mr. Younger called out from the parlor. "But are you prepared to eat in the dark?"

"No!" the boy said.

"Then you'd better stay where you are and behave yourself," Mr. Younger responded.

"Your tutor starts next week," Winnie reminded the boy. "He'll be having lunch with us. He won't want to work with you if you keep on stuffing food in your mouth and spilling things."

"Perhaps," Grandmother said quietly, "Clare can give Jackie a few private lessons in the kitchen."

"We'll eat with Mrs. Klacker," Clare said, smiling at the boy. "You'll like that."

"No," Jackie said, and he tore off his napkin and left the room, with Tip at his heels.

The boarders finished their coffee, thanked Grandmother for sharing Bonnie's letter, and left the table. Clare looked around at the women in her family. "I think this problem with Jackie's table manners should be handled another time, and more discreetly, too," she said. "No one likes being corrected in public."

"You're right," Grandmother said. "We aren't used to having boys around."

"You never have classes for boys at Neighborhood House, do you?" Clare asked.

Winnie said, "No," and Grandmother added that boys were never interested in anything the place had to offer.

"I seldom see them in the library after they're much older than Jackie," Mama said.

"They're too busy derailing the streetcars," Winnie said.

The women laughed, but uneasily. Jackie was the first boy who had ever lived in the house.

Clare, who was writing a diary letter of her own to Bonnie, and waiting to mail it until Bonnie arrived finally at the mission, added a few lines that night repeating the dinner time conversation.

What do you make of this? Boys are unknown to us
and to the Neighborhood House. Jackie is a mystery.
I hope we do him good and not harm.

That night, she dreamed of Bonnie and Hawaii. In her dream, they walked on those beautiful beaches. But then, suddenly, Bonnie was gone! Clare woke with a start and sat up in bed.

Bonnie was far away, too far to ask if she was all right.

She realized that Tip was standing in her doorway, his head cocked. She could see him in a patch of moonlight, watching her. She must have cried out and awakened the dog.

"It's all right," she told him. As if he understood her, the dog went back to Jackie's room.

Bonnie, be safe, Clare thought.

12

On the Fourth of July, Clare and Marietta took Jackie and Sarah downtown to the parade. Late in the hot afternoon, they brought the children back to the boarding house for the picnic Mrs. Klacker prepared for them on the shady porch. The youngsters had developed an odd friendship, which involved almost no talking. Clare wondered if they read each other's mind.

At nine the following morning, Jackie's tutor arrived for the first time. Mr. John Dallas was a young assistant professor from the University of Washington, whom Grandmother had met once at a lecture.

He was unusually tall, with dark curling hair and friendly dark eyes. Jackie regarded him with alarm, and when Grandmother suggested that he and Mr. Dallas go into the library and begin their lessons, Jackie turned pale and backed up, reaching down to touch Tip for comfort.

"Perhaps we could sit outside on the porch," Mr. Dallas suggested easily. "It's a pleasant morning. We would be quite comfortable there. And, of course, we'll want the dog with us."

The look of relief on Jackie's face was enough for Grandmother. "Clare will bring you anything you need," she said. "And Jackie, Clare will be sitting right inside if you should want anything."

Mr. Dallas smiled at Clare. "She's welcome to sit with us this first time," he said.

Jackie's pleading look was not wasted on Clare. "I'll stay for a while," she told the man. She was curious to see how he would tutor the boy.

"I understand you will be wearing glasses shortly," Mr. Dallas said to Jackie, and before the boy could answer, he took his own out of the inside pocket of his jacket and put them on. "There, that's better," he said. "I don't like it when I can't see clearly. My brother wears his glasses even when he rides his horse."

Jackie stared at him, open-mouthed. "Is he a cowboy?"

"No, but he lives in the country and keeps a horse to ride on weekends. I have a very good book about horses, which I'll bring to you as soon as you have your glasses. Now. Why don't you tell me what you were doing in school when you were there last?"

Jackie, drawing invisible circles on the table with his forefinger, said, "We were doing sums. And we were reading a story about a boy named Bob who rescued a boy named Tim in a flood."

"I know that story," Mr. Dallas said. "In fact, I have that book at home, too. I'll bring it with me in a few days. But right now, let's talk about the sums you were doing."

"Well," Jackie began earnestly, "I remember them pretty good."

Clare smiled. This was going to work, because Mr. Dallas understood children. Grandmother and Winnie would be pleased.

Another letter from Bonnie arrived.

Miss Edgars was right. I actually could smell Yokohama when we were still out to sea. Miss Edgars says that I must accustom myself to the different standards of hygiene in Asia, but it's hard not to think of the diseases that are associated with the awful smell of sewage and rotting garbage. We spent a day in the city, and I saw much that was

beautiful. It's very crowded, with small houses made
of wood jammed together, but I caught glimpses of
many pretty gardens, some no larger than tablecloths.
We went back to the ship for dinner, and tomorrow
we set out to sea again. The next stop will be China.

"She's having a wonderful time," Mrs. Carver said
after Grandmother finished reading the letter.

"She's having the adventure of a lifetime," Mama said.

Suddenly everyone at the table turned to look at
Clare. "You'll be next," Winnie said. "You'll be surpris-
ing us one of these days."

Clare looked down at her dessert plate, wondering
how disappointed Winnie would be if she suspected
that while Clare might envy Bonnie, she did not want
what Bonnie had chosen.

But what do I want? she thought. Why don't I have
the sense of purpose Bonnie had when she was sixteen?
What's wrong with me?

Jackie received his glasses the following week. He came
home looking like a sober little owl, and went straight
upstairs to his room. Clare, worried, followed him.

"How do you like your glasses?" she asked him from
the door of his room.

He sat at the foot of is bed with Tip next to him. "I look like a sissy," he said sadly.

"But how was it when you first put them on?" Clare asked. "When you looked around, what did you see?"

He raised his head and suddenly smiled. "I saw... things! Things everywhere! And everything is...is... bright! There are colors and signs with words and pictures on them and" —he dug in his pocket and took out a penny— "and I found this on the street, and Miss Devereaux said I mustn't touch it, but Mrs. Devereaux said I could if I didn't put my fingers in my mouth afterward and washed my hands when I got home."

"Then let's wash them right now," Clare said. "And we'll wash the penny too. It can be your lucky penny." Inwardly, she was practically singing. He loves being able to see well, she thought. He'll wear his glasses. Mr. Dallas thinks he's very intelligent. What might he be able to learn, now that he can see!

And then she remembered Mr. Younger, who never stopped learning even after he could no longer see.

A few days later, Clare joined Marietta, her mother, and her sister, Sarah, on a short trip to a small lake near Seattle, where the Nelsons owned a rough cabin. It had only one room, with two sets of bunk beds, a cot, and a table and chairs. But outside, on the broad porch, comfortable wicker furniture overlooked the lake on one side and a summer kitchen on the other. Clare had spent time there before, on weekdays when Mr. Nelson was still in the city, and she had enjoyed her visits. There were several other cabins nearby, and the mothers and children spent most of their time outdoors.

The first afternoon, when the girls followed a narrow path around the lake, Marietta said, "I told Mama that I wanted to go to New York when I finish high school."

"You're serious about it, then," Clare said, surprised.

"Of course," Marietta said. Her face was red. "Not that it will do me any good. Mama only laughed at me. She said I had a duty to Pa and her to settle down with a husband and raise a family." Marietta bent to pick up a rock and threw it angrily into the lake. "On my birthday, my aunt and uncle are bringing a young man from Uncle's firm to meet me."

Clare shook her head, mystified. "What for?"

"They didn't say so, but I know they hope I'll be interested in him and he'll be interested in me, and then I'll get married and they won't have to worry about me anymore. They talk about Bonnie a lot, about how wild she is and—"

"Wild!" Clare exclaimed. "Bonnie has never done a wild thing in her whole life."

173

"She's gone to China," Marietta said. "My mother thinks the Chinese live in caves and hunt with spears."

"You don't have to marry this man," Clare said. "You don't even know him. You might hate him."

"Then they'll just find someone else," Marietta said. "My aunt said they know half a dozen young men who would be suitable, and Pa says there's someone new coming into his office in September."

"This sounds like something out of a book," Clare said disgustedly. "I can't believe that your parents want to arrange a marriage for you."

"Their marriage was arranged. So was my aunt's. Mama says lots of nice people make sure their daughters are 'settled' with the right man."

The day was warm, but Clare, chilled, hugged herself. "No one can make you marry if you don't want to do it," she said.

Marietta threw another rock. "What would you do?" she asked.

"Tell them I won't meet those men and I won't get married," Clare said.

"But you wouldn't run away," Marietta said.

"I wouldn't have to," Clare said. "I just wouldn't do it."

Marietta sighed. "You don't understand what it's like when your family wants you to do a certain thing and never stops nagging. After a while, it's easier to do what they say. After a while, you get tired of fighting about it."

"Marietta!" Clare exclaimed. "That doesn't sound like you."

"I don't know what sounds like me, because I don't know what I want. Not for certain, anyway."

And neither do I, Clare thought.

After three days at the cabin, Clare left the Nelsons behind and returned to find that Carson Younger's mother was at the boarding house. She lived in Portland, and came to visit her son occasionally, sharing Clare's room if Bonnie wasn't there or sleeping in the extra bed in Mrs. Carver's room.

"When did you get here?" Clare asked, smiling at Mrs. Younger as soon as she saw her.

Mrs. Younger was setting the table in the dining room for tea. She made herself useful whenever she spent time in Seattle. The woman looked up and flushed a little.

"Clare, here you are," she said. "I arrived this morning."

"Are you staying upstairs with me or are you in with Mrs. Carver?" Clare asked.

"Actually, dear, I'm leaving on an evening train," she said. She busied herself with napkins.

"You're going back home already?" Clare asked.

"Clare, dear, you're home," Grandmother said as she came in through the pantry's swinging door. "Did you have a good time?"

"The lake was lovely," Clare said. "Are we letting Mrs. Younger leave the same day she arrives? What will Mr. Younger think of us?"

"He and his mother had a surprise for us," Grandmother said as she put down a platter of Mrs. Klacker's special tea sandwiches.

"Oh, egg salad!" Clare said delightedly. "Wonderful. But what's the surprise?" She looked over at Mrs. Younger and saw the woman biting her lower lip. "What's wrong? I can tell that something's wrong."

"Nothing's wrong," Mrs. Younger said smoothly. "Carson shouldn't keep secrets as well as he does, I'm afraid. He and I are going to New York for a month. I came up to help him a little, although he hates it when I fuss. But we'll be on our way this evening."

Clare, who had been about to pick up one of the small sandwiches, stopped. "But why?" she asked.

"That's exactly what I asked," Grandmother said. She carried cups and saucers from the sideboard and set

176

them down at the head of the table. "Why New York at this time of year? I've heard it's very warm there."

"This was the only good time for us," Mrs. Younger said. "I have a month free and so does Carson, so it seemed a terrible waste not to take advantage of it."

"It must be very exciting," Clare said. "Marietta wants to go—" She stopped speaking abruptly.

Grandmother and Mrs. Younger didn't seem to notice.

"I envy you the plays and concerts you'll be enjoying," Grandmother said. "Now. Shall we find everybody and tell them tea is ready?"

Mrs. Carver came downstairs first. "Clare, did you have a wonderful time?"

Clare nodded, distracted, waiting for Mr. Younger to come into the dining room. When his mother was there, he would have tea with the rest of the people in the house. Her presence relieved him of some of his self-consciousness.

Jackie came in from the yard, greeted Clare with a big smile, and ran upstairs to wash his hands. Mrs. Klacker brought in the teapot, eyed Clare closely, and said, "Don't they feed you out at that lake? You look as if you haven't had a decent meal since you left."

It was good to be home again, but something was

wrong. She could feel it in the air, like a cold mist. But Grandmother and the others seemed oblivious. It was only Mrs. Younger who could not meet her eyes.

Mr. Younger came in then. Tip ran to meet him and barked once. The man bent to pat him, then said, "I heard Clare's voice."

"I'm here," she said. "Your mother told me that the two of you are leaving for New York this evening."

He extended his cane and tapped his way to the table. "Tea is ready?" he asked. "Ah. Shall I sit here?"

Mrs. Klacker came back in, this time carrying cream and lemon slices. "Sit wherever you like, dearie. Since this is your last tea with us for a while, I made you a special treat."

"Not lemon curd?" he said as he sat down.

"Two layers of it on a nice puff pastry," Mrs. Klacker said, and she went off to the kitchen again.

Jackie came in, wiping his hands on his pants. "Aren't we having crackers and jam?" he called after the woman.

"Yes, yes, yes," she called back.

Any other time, Clare would have been pleased and amused at the comfortable gathering together of the people in the house for afternoon tea. But today, uneasiness caused her to fidget.

However, the conversation at the table was pleasant, although rather vague when the Youngers were asked about their travel plans. Mr. Younger asked many questions about the Nelsons' place at the lake, and Clare thought that he didn't care so much about the answers as about keeping her talking.

Mr. Reynolds came home early from his office and announced that his car was waiting to take the Youngers to the train station.

Winnie rushed in then, out of breath. "I'm not too late. Good! I brought you a few things for the train, chocolates and the newest magazines, and—" She thrust packages at Mrs. Younger, then sobered. "Oh, dear. Mr. Younger, we shall miss your snarls from the small parlor every evening."

"And I shall miss your latest accounts of the war on ignorance," the young man assured her.

"Why can't anyone in this house take railroad schedules seriously?" Mr. Reynolds complained. "Are the suitcases downstairs? Is anyone ready to leave, or shall I go by myself?"

Everyone deserted the table at once to help. Mama and Mr. Partridge came in before Mr. Reynolds succeeded in getting the travelers out the door. More goodbyes were said, and Clare, with Jackie and Tip beside her, watched the auto drive away.

"Tip feels real bad," Jackie observed as the auto turned the corner.

"So do I," Clare said, almost to herself.

Jackie looked up at her. "You like him a lot, don't you?" he asked.

Clare sighed. "Yes."

"So do I," Jackie said. He reached for Clare's hand. "You could read the paper to me," he said. "I'll listen."

"Thank you," Clare said.

Winnie came up behind them. "Don't you wonder what they're really up to?" she asked.

Clare had difficulty sleeping that night, and at two o'clock, she came downstairs to the kitchen to fix a cup of tea. While she waited for the tea to brew, she stepped out on the side porch, and heard a new sound from the Tree of Bells. There had been five bells hanging from it before she left for the lake, each one with a different voice, but now she heard a new sound.

He put up another bell before he left, she thought, listening.

What does he want?

13

Not one of Marietta's friends was invited to her birthday dinner. It was the first time Clare had ever been excluded from this family occasion, but Marietta's explanation made Clare laugh.

"It's because they've invited that fellow they think will be my future husband," Marietta said disgustedly. "Mama told me that if you came, he might be distracted from me. I wish you would come, even if you aren't invited. I can't think of anything I'd like better than to have him fall madly in love with somebody."

"Don't count on me for that," Clare said.

They sat in the shade on the side porch, fanning themselves with magazines. The vines that curled over the porch railing barely stirred in a light afternoon breeze. Jackie and Tip napped on the porch swing. Inside, barely audible, Grandmother and Mrs. Klacker talked while they polished the glass doors on the dining room china cupboard.

"The only good part of this whole silly birthday situation is that Mama said I could invite my friends from school to lunch downtown, anywhere I like. So naturally I chose the Olympic Hotel dining room. I thought for a second that Mama was going to faint. But she kept her word and made the reservations for all the girls in our class."

"Don't tell Grandmother," Clare cautioned. "She'll want to do that for me next year."

"I'll tell her about the family dinner, and maybe she'll find a suitable young man for you."

Clare shook her head slowly. "No. I know she wouldn't do that."

"Because you've already picked the suitable young man yourself, haven't you?" Marietta asked.

Clare closed her eyes for a moment and took a deep breath. "For all the good it will do me," she said. "He thinks I'm a child. And he'll probably love Bonnie for the rest of his life."

"Mr. Younger," Marietta said with satisfaction. "I knew it. When he comes back from New York, why don't you hint around about how you feel?"

"You really are a strange girl," Clare said, laughing. "Can you imagine what he'd say?"

"I can imagine it, all right," Marietta said. "And it's wonderful."

"Idiot," Clare said.

"And he'd probably say that, too," Marietta said.

Their laughter woke Jackie, who sat up, yawning, and asked if dinner was ready yet. Disappointed to learn that it wasn't, he wandered inside to beg a snack from Mrs. Klacker. Tip jumped back up on the swing.

"Here's the mailman," Marietta said. "Maybe you'll get another letter from Bonnie today."

Clare met the man at the mailbox and took the mail from him. "You're right," she told Marietta. "Here's a nice thick letter from her."

"China," Marietta breathed. "She's so lucky. But I'll settle for New York."

Grandmother read the letter aloud to the girls immediately.

> *Seeing China for the first time overwhelmed me. It was raining hard when our ship entered the Yangtze estuary, but in spite of the rain, there were little wooden boats everywhere, with whole families dressed in loose blue cotton pants and tunics, and wearing hats made of bamboo slats. They went about their business*

aboard as if not a drop was falling. I saw several destroyers, too, both American and British. The shoreline is crowded with docks and ships, and in between, there are more dilapidated shacks and warehouses than anyone could count.

We turned into the Whangpo, and there was Shanghai. The rain stopped for a few minutes, and Miss Edgars pointed out the most important buildings that were visible from the water. Below the buildings, there was such a jumble of tiny shops and stalls, crooked roads and rickshaws, that I was certain I could never sort things out. But Miss Edgars wasn't intimidated. It's all as familiar to her as Seattle is to me.

Mr. Reynolds' friends, the Sydneys, were waiting for us, and invited us to stay with them in the International sector, where they have a home, but Miss Edgars insisted that we go to the mission house in the city, because we were expected there. I think she disapproves of the wealthy Americans here. The mission provided us with a small, clean room. In spite of Miss Edgars' frowns, I spent several pleasant days with the Sydneys and some of the people we met on the voyage. I had nothing better to do, since our journey up river was delayed because the Yangtze had flooded. *The weather is hard to bear. Rain falls in great sheets part of the time, and the rest of the time the humidity is stifling. And it's hot. Finally we left Shanghai, on a much smaller ship than the one on which we arrived, and set off for Nanking. Then our real adventures began.*

Scarcely two hours out, we passed an American gunboat heading toward Shanghai, and a young American sailor called out to me. "Are you British? American?" he shouted. "American!" I shouted back. (Miss Edgars nearly choked over this.) "I'm from Washington State," he shouted. "Seattle." "So am I!" I yelled at the top of my lungs. "What's your name?" he yelled. But by that time we were too far apart. What a thrill, though, to find someone from home.

That was the last pleasant event on the voyage.

Late in the afternoon, we passed a village where all the people had come out and were standing in two lines in a large open place not far from the dock. There were many armed men in uniform standing guard, and one small fellow with a sword seemed to be in charge. In the center of the two lines, I saw a heavy-set man with a broader unsheathed sword, several kneeling people, and round things I first thought were dark melons of some sort, but Miss

Edgars said, "Lord save us, he's beheaded them!" I thought my heart had stopped.

As we sailed past, the man with the sword turned to look at us but apparently found us of no interest because he turned his back on us immediately. Our boat sailed on. Only Miss Edgars and I were upset. The Chinese on board seemed to be blind to the hideous scene. "Who was that?" I asked Miss Edgars. "It's Chiang," she said. "One of the young generals in the Kuomintang. He must believe that the villagers have supported one of the other warlords. He executes every tenth person he finds, even women and children. There's always trouble along the river. There's even a gang of pirates led by an American woman. She's only twenty-one, and her family lives in Shanghai. She actually attacks the gunboats." I could hardly believe this.

Miss Edgars speaks Mandarin and two dialects, and so she could talk with the other passengers, who, she assured me, were not concerned about their safety. I felt better after we reached Nanking. Tomorrow we leave by train for the mission. Miss Edgars says that we will be completely safe, so I am assuring all of you that you must not worry. I've told you the worst thing I saw and now I'll tell you the best things.

I saw two small boys herding a hundred fat

ducks down a narrow road between beautiful farms.
I saw women dressed in gorgeous embroidered silks,
and they didn't seem to mind that their feet had been
bound and crippled, perhaps because their exquisite
shoes were made of satin and embroidered with pearls.
Miss Edgars tells me that small feet are desired by
all the women. Only the poorest peasant women have
unbound feet.

I'll write more on the train. Now, my dears, write
to me at the mission and tell me what you have been
doing this summer.

After Grandmother put the letter aside to read to the
boarders after dinner, Clare walked Marietta home.

"When I'm in New York, I'll send you diary letters,"
Marietta said. "They won't be that exciting — I mean,
where would I see beheaded bodies! — but maybe I'll
succeed in persuading you to join me there. Wouldn't
we have fun?"

Clare shook her head slowly. "I might come for a visit, but this is where I belong."

"Someday it will be," Marietta said. "But first, don't
you want to try something different? Don't you want to
see another part of the world?"

Clare could imagine seeing other parts of the world,
but only for brief visits.

"I think we are going in different directions," she told Marietta. "And it makes me sad."

"Don't be sad," Marietta said. "We can't be girls forever."

She was right, of course.

Clare thought of Mr. Younger constantly. She tried to imagine what he was doing and where he was. And when he was coming back. She missed him more than she could have thought possible. But the others in the house missed him, too, and he was always discussed during dinner.

"I wonder what Mr. Younger would think about the contaminated milk scandal," Mr. Partridge mused one evening. "Eleven children dead and twenty more in the hospital. It's an outrage."

"Oh, he'd want someone strung up from a lamp post," Mr. Reynolds said.

"What will Mr. Younger think about Tip's new tricks?" Mrs. Carver said another time.

"We're going to surprise him," Jackie said proudly. "We can hardly wait until he gets back."

Clare caught Grandmother looking at her that time, her delicate eyebrows lifted. Clare's face burned.

Marietta's birthday dinner was a disaster, by her own design. That morning she cut off her hair and did such a terrible job that her mother had no choice but to send her downtown to a hairdresser to have the ragged ends trimmed off. Marietta had insisted that Clare go with her, and Clare watched while her friend's beautiful red hair was cut into a bob as short as a boy's.

When they left the hairdresser, Marietta insisted that they stop for tea. "Mama will be frantic, wondering where we are," Marietta said with satisfaction. "If I stay away long enough, maybe she'll understand that I won't put up with being paraded around in front of young men like a piece of meat. One more year, Clare, and I'll be free."

The next morning, Marietta walked in only minutes after the men in the house had left for work. Her grin told the story, but she pulled Clare into Mr. Younger's little parlor and supplied the details.

"That fellow my aunt and uncle brought was awful," she said. "But by the time I was through, he thought I was the biggest disaster since the San Francisco earthquake."

"I'm afraid to ask what you did," Clare said.

"Before or after I spilled my water in my uncle's lap?" Marietta asked. "Or would you like to hear how I dipped my bread in my gravy?"

"You did not," Clare said.

"I did. And—" Marietta began laughing so hard that she couldn't speak, so Clare had to wait until she had control of herself again. "And," she said, wiping her eyes, "when the meal was done, I looked around and belched. Remember how we used to have contests to see who could belch the loudest?"

"When we were in second grade!" Clare protested. "And Miss Levant made us write 'I will be a lady,' a hundred times on the blackboard."

"I was the champion then and I haven't lost the knack," Marietta said proudly. "I thought Auntie would be sick. She actually turned green. But I wiped my mouth on my hand and said, 'Sorry, folks,' just like the good girl I am."

"You are anything but a good girl," Clare said. "What did your parents do?"

"Mama cried and Pa took my spending money away until September," Marietta said. "But after everyone went to bed last night, Sarah came into my room and told me that she was glad I did it. She said she wished she was that brave."

Marietta's party with her friends at the Olympic Hotel, however, was a great success, and it was mentioned on the society pages of all three of Seattle's newspapers. Mrs. Nelson almost forgave her daughter for her behavior at the dinner, because the photograph in two of the papers showed her, the mother, at her best.

That evening at dinner, Winnie showed one of the newspapers to the boarders and asked them what they thought Mr. Younger might have said about the photo.

"We could describe it to him when he returns," Mr. Partridge said.

"We had better not," Grandmother advised. "He is not fond of the Nelsons, except for Marietta, and he thinks society pages should be banned. He calls them obscene."

Everyone at the table laughed, but Clare had to clench her fists tightly to keep tears from her eyes. Oh, she missed him so much.

Mr. Younger sent Mr. Reynolds a telegram one day and asked that his friend pick him up at the train station on the following Friday. The telegram contained no other information.

Mrs. Klacker prepared Mr. Younger's favorite summer meal, cold fried chicken, potato salad, and buttermilk biscuits. Winnie cut two great bouquets of roses for the small sitting room. Jackie rehearsed Tip in his new tricks. Everyone was waiting on the porch when the men arrived.

"But where is your mother?" Grandmother asked Mr. Younger as soon as everyone had greeted him and Tip had barked and howled at Jackie's commands.

"She left the train in Portland," Mr. Younger said. "I think she's had enough of me for now."

Clare thought that he looked thinner. His dark glasses were different, too. And he wore a new summer suit.

He's so handsome, she thought. But he looks tired.

"Did you have a good trip on the train?" she asked.

He turned to face her and smiled. "I wouldn't want to make another long trip so soon," he said. "I'm glad to be back. Tell me what you've been doing since I left, Clare."

"Nothing much," she said.

"Oh, nonsense," Winnie interrupted. "She's been working nearly every day at the Neighborhood House, and she has made plans to teach a class of boys this winter."

"A class of boys," Mr. Younger said. "What on earth could you teach boys?"

"How to care for their pets," she said. He thought she

was an idiot, of course. Probably he was laughing at her.

"She came up with that idea herself," Grandmother said proudly. "We've been trying to think of something that would lure boys to us, and Clare remembered how much pleasure Jackie gets from caring for Tip, so she's planned a class. She even consulted with a veterinarian. He's quite taken with our Clare."

"Grandmother!" Clare exclaimed. "Wherever did you get an idea like that?"

"I assumed it, since he has found a dozen reasons to telephone you since you first went to see him," Grandmother said composedly.

Clare stared at her grandmother. "He called twice, once to ask me if I would like copies of a magazine about dogs and then to tell me that he had located a few copies."

Winnie's face was purple. "Audra! You surely aren't encouraging him to have hopes about Clare!" she sputtered. "Why, she's only a child."

"She is not a child and I am not encouraging him to do anything," Grandmother said. She excused herself and got up from the table. "I'll bring in more coffee," she said.

Winnie and Clare stared at each other. "I think the heat's gotten to her," Winnie said.

Clare saw, to her humiliation, that Mr. Younger was

wearing his wry, half-smile, which meant that he had found something in the conversation that had entertained him.

She followed her grandmother into the kitchen. "Grandmother, that was awful," she said. "You sounded like Mrs. Nelson."

Grandmother, pouring coffee from the percolator into the silver coffee pot, said, "I certainly did not."

"What possessed you to try matchmaking?" Clare demanded.

Mrs. Klacker, cutting pieces of blackberry pie, hooted with laughter.

"I was merely satisfying my curiosity," Grandmother said. "I wondered if it's true, that absence makes the heart grow fonder."

Clare gritted her teeth. "I'll satisfy your curiosity," she said. "Yes, I like him even better than I did before. And no, he doesn't like me any better. He's dying for the chance to throw what you said in my face and tease me until I cry. I can't understand why you're trying to push me at him. You would hate it if I said I wanted to marry instead of go to college. Wouldn't you? Wouldn't you?"

"No one said anything about getting married any time soon," Grandmother said. "But I have always hated having things hang over my head."

She started out the door to the pantry, but Clare was right behind her.

"Like a noose?" she asked.

Grandmother went on serenely through the swinging door to the dining room, where Mr. Younger was entertaining the other boarders with stories about New York.

Frustrated, Clare looked around at them. They had already forgotten what had embarrassed her so much.

Except for Jackie. Bewildered, he stared at her.

She smiled and tousled his hair. "Would you like to sit out on the porch with me?" she said. "It's very warm in here."

Jackie and Tip followed her out, and sat with her on the top step. The sun was setting, and the western sky was rose and gold.

"It's nice when everything stays the same, isn't it?" Jackie said.

Summer ended and cool weather returned at last. Jackie loved his new school and made two close friends, although Sarah remained a frequent visitor, now that Mr. Partridge was teaching the youngsters to play chess. Marietta's new hairstyle was a great success at the Academy. Clare's pet care class attracted the attention of seven boys, to her astonishment, and another five boys signed up for the next one.

There were times that autumn when Clare thought that Mr. Younger had changed toward her. He was less sarcastic, and he finally abandoned teasing her. But instead, he had taken to grilling her about her plans at Neighborhood House, and often he criticized her until she was furious.

"One of these days you'll tell me that when you go to the university you'll study to be a social worker," he said.

"No, I won't," she answered. "But I've heard that they teach classes in homemaking skills, and I think—"

"My god, you have lost your mind," Mr. Younger said. "Why would you do that? If you want to learn to cook, go ask Mrs. Klacker. She would be the best teacher you could find."

Clare blinked. "You wouldn't care?"

"Why should I care, may I ask?" he demanded. "Someday you'll marry. Probably your future husband would prefer that you learned to make a meal that would not result in his painful and immediate death."

Clare scowled. "You needn't be so insulting," she said. "I'm not like Bonnie. I don't want to do the things Bonnie has done. I want my own life."

"What life is that?" he demanded.

She was silent for a moment, and then she burst into tears. "I really hate you," she said, and she ran out of the parlor.

The next time she saw him, he said, "What are you wearing?"

"A flour sack," she grumbled.

"You little brat," he replied, and he laughed.

Clare stormed off and nearly bumped into Grandmother, who was coming into the room. Grandmother was smiling.

"Oh!" Clare cried and she ran upstairs.

Winter brought an early, heavy snow, along with the usual holiday plans. Mrs. Younger traveled from Portland to join them for Christmas, and she gave Clare a beautiful silver clip, inlaid with mother-of-pearl. Clare gave her a framed sketch she had made of Mr. Younger with Tip on his lap.

Mr. Younger gave Clare a journal bound in blue leather. When she thanked him, he said, "I want you to wait to write in it until you graduate from high school in June."

"Why?" she asked.

"Because life grows more interesting then," he said.

One evening in January, while Clare read to Mr. Younger about the marvels discovered in King Tut's tomb, a messenger brought a cable to the door. It was addressed to Grandmother.

After the he left, Grandmother stood in the hall holding the cable, her face pale.

"Something must be wrong," Winnie said. "Open it, Audra."

"Is it from Bonnie?" Mama asked.

But Grandmother only stood here, frozen, with the cable in her hand.

Mr. Partridge took it from her hand. "May I?" he asked, and without waiting for her answer, he opened the envelope and read from the small sheet of yellow paper:

BONNIE SHASTER ONLY SURVIVOR DEPARTED SHANGHAI QUEEN MAUD JANUARY 10 STOP ACCOMPANIED BY MRS. OLIVER CAMPBELL STOP. WILL ARRIVE SAN FRANCISCO 26 STOP CONDITION REMAINS SERIOUS STOP REVEREND ARWIN BELLAMY

There was a moment of terrible silence, and then Mama cried, "What does it mean?"

"Wire the doctor who owns the boarding house where Bonnie was living," Mr. Younger said quickly.

"The mission doctor is his cousin. He must know what is going on."

Mr. Reynolds hurried to the phone, and they listened while he called Western Union and directed a message to the Berkeley boarding house. He knew the address, of course. He had written Bonnie many times. When he was done, he walked past them as if they were invisible, and sat down in the darkened front parlor.

"My god," Clare heard him say.

The first reply came the next morning. The doctor had heard nothing about his cousin in China. But later in the morning, he sent another telegram, and that one brought terrible news.

The mission had been attacked by one of the dozens of small armies warring in China. Only Bonnie survived. She had been shot in the back and left for dead with the others. Sympathetic farmers had found her and sent her by train to Nanking, where she was treated by an American doctor, moved to Shanghai, and then put aboard a ship. The woman accompanying her was the American doctor's wife, a nurse.

Their Bonnie was injured and in the care of strangers.

Later that afternoon, Clare sat alone in the dining room, watching rain fall outside, her mind a jumble of fears.

"She's strong," Mr. Younger said, startling her.

Clare had not heard him come into the room.

"And she is focused on the future," he went on. "People like that survive almost anything."

He left then, calling Tip to accompany him, and they retreated to his lair.

Later, Clare wondered how he had known she was in the dining room.

14

Mr. Reynolds' friend at the steamship company tried to help. He sent a radio message to the *Queen Maud*, asking for a report on Bonnie's condition, and called the family late one evening to tell them that the ship's doctor had replied that Bonnie was resting comfortably.

"Whatever that's supposed to mean," Mr. Reynolds said grimly.

"I doubt if they would have let her board if she had been in critical condition," Mr. Partridge said.

"Let's consider the message from the doctor to be good news," Winnie said, but she was so nervous she was wringing her hands.

Mrs. Klacker served tea, offering a cup to Grandmother first, but Grandmother did not see her until the cook spoke her name.

Mr. Younger, Jackie, and Tip sat before the fire in the

small back parlor, silent and sad. Clare saw Mrs. Klacker put a piece of the old Ornament Tree on the fire, and she was not certain whether this was an omen of good or evil.

The house was unnaturally quiet during the next few days. The ship's doctor sent a brief line every other day, but the message never changed: Bonnie rested comfortably.

The family and the boarders counted the days. Then, abruptly, Grandmother and Mr. Reynolds decided to meet Bonnie's ship in San Francisco.

"If necessary, we'll bring her home to Seattle," Grandmother said. "But I hope she will be well when she arrives, and after a good rest, she can go back to her studies."

Clare was not as optimistic as Grandmother. Sometimes she dreamed about Bonnie, terrible dreams that jolted her awake. She kept this to herself, for Grandmother's sake.

Once, late in the evening, Clare went into Mr. Younger's parlor and asked if she could speak to him confidentially.

He had been reading, but he put his Braille book aside and invited her to sit down. "Is this about Bonnie?" he asked gently.

Clare sat down next to him. "Tell me what it's like to be shot," she whispered.

"I don't know personally," he said. "I was injured by the blast of the shell, and I wasn't aware of anything until I woke up in the hospital. But I saw many men shot. I'm speaking to you frankly, because you wouldn't have come in here on your own unless you were desperate."

"You make it sound as if I never come in here unless you ask me," Clare said, hurt beyond tears because he seemed to be reprimanding her for an offense at such a terrible time.

"You never come in. Not anymore. I've wondered — No matter." He brushed back his hair and seemed suddenly puzzled. "What did you ask me, dear?"

Clare looked away, then back at him. "You saw men shot? Do they lose consciousness right away, or do they know —"

"Some lose consciousness," Mr. Younger said evenly. "Some suffer. Is that what you wanted to know? If Bonnie suffered? I don't know. Pain is strange. After it's over, we can't remember it exactly. We can't recreate it. It's not like remembering the scent of a lemon and having your mouth water. There are few mercies in this life, but one is our inability to turn the memory of pain into a reality."

Clare was silent for a long time. Mr. Younger waited patiently.

"Do you think she will be all right?" Clare asked finally.

"Yes. Your grandmother and Nicholas will see to that. She will go back to school and then to medical school, and her life will be exactly as she had planned, except for one thing. Now she knows the worst that humans are capable of. Her natural compassion will intensify. The good among us become better after something like this."

Clare reached out and took his hand in hers. "Thank you," she whispered.

He placed his other hand over hers and would not let her go. "Stay with me for a while," he said.

Stunned, Clare sat very still. And then she realized that the light had been on when she came into the room.

"You weren't sitting here in the dark when I came in," she said.

"No," he said. Suddenly he let go of her hand and stood up. "Is Mrs. Klacker still in the kitchen?"

"Can I get something for you?" Clare asked.

"She'll take care of it," he said. He picked up his cane and tapped out of the room, leaving her behind.

Three days before Grandmother and Mr. Reynolds planned to leave for San Francisco, Grandmother received a cable from Mrs. Campbell, the woman who had accompanied Bonnie from Shanghai. Bonnie had developed pneumonia during the voyage, and had left the ship in Honolulu. She was in a hospital there.

Mr. Reynolds did not hesitate. He contacted his friend at the steamship company immediately and arranged passage for himself and Grandmother on the next ship leaving for Hawaii. They sailed two days later.

"This nightmare will never end," Clare said when she and Winnie returned to the house after saying goodbye to the voyagers.

"Yes it will, love," Mrs. Klacker said. "There are six new bells on the tree."

Grandmother wrote every day after she reached Bonnie. Her letters were read aloud at dinner to the boarders, so everyone could share the news. Gradually, Bonnie improved, but weeks passed before she was strong enough to leave her bed. On Clare's seventeenth birthday, she received a birthday card from Bonnie, whose handwriting was nearly illegible. But Clare passed the card around the dinner table, and everyone was pleased at Bonnie's steady improvement.

Clare's birthday was not celebrated, at her insistence, but her family and Marietta gave her small gifts. And Mr. Younger, smiling wickedly, gave her a cookbook, which made her laugh for the first time since the cable arrived.

Then, one day near the end of March, a letter came from Bonnie herself:

> *Audra, Reginald, and I are leaving for San Francisco tomorrow. Audra will stay in Berkeley with me for a while, although I'm strong enough to take care of myself now. But you know how she is. I miss you all, and think about you.*

"Well, that was cryptic," Winnie said.

"Is Mr. Reynolds coming back to Seattle with Grandmother?" Clare asked.

"She didn't say," Mama said.

Jackie, who had listened to the letter while spreading jam on crackers, said, "I s'pose he's staying in California with Bonnie, to keep her from getting shot again."

Clare burst out laughing, and then blushed because Jackie's observation was not meant to be amusing. The child had been quite serious.

"Jackie might be right," Mrs. Carver said slowly, thoughtfully. "Not that Bonnie is in any danger in

Berkeley. But Mr. Reynolds might want to stay nearby."

"But Bonnie won't have time for him," Winnie protested. "She's ambitious. She has her future all planned."

"Perhaps she has plans we don't know anything about," Mr. Partridge said. "Well, I say this is a perfect solution. With him around, we won't need to worry about Bonnie. But I will miss him at the bridge table."

Later, Clare realized that by losing Mr. Reynolds, the family would be losing part of their income. A new boarder would have to be found, someone compatible with the others.

Money. It was always a problem. The roof needed to be replaced. The house was starting to look shabby, and new paint was in order. In less than three months, Clare would be graduating from high school. How would she get the money for her college tuition? She did not have an inheritance like Bonnie's. Her grandmother would tell her not to worry, but how could she not worry? Instead of being prepared to work, her school had only prepared her for college. Or marriage.

She had not heard from her father at Christmas, but he often forgot the holiday. She still had his old address, so she sat down that night to write him a frank letter. She asked him if he could help them financially, and then, so that he would not feel that she was blaming him for anything, she added,

I'm certain you would help if you could, but if you
cannot, then I will understand. I hope, as always,
that you are well.

Your daughter, Clare

She mailed the letter the next day on the way to school, and said nothing about it to anyone. When she did not receive an answer, she was not surprised.

Grandmother returned to Seattle at the end of April, so glad to be home that she refused to sit down for the first few minutes, but walked around the house, inside and out, as if greeting an old friend. Winnie decorated the dining room table with lilacs, and Mrs. Klacker produced a feast.

"I am so glad to see all of you," Grandmother said when she sat down. "Now I am going to answer the questions I'm certain you all have uppermost on your minds. How is Bonnie? She is gaining strength every day, but she is not as well as she would like everyone to believe. Will Mr. Reynolds return to us here? No. We will pack up his things and ship them to San Francisco. He already has found a pleasant small apartment overlooking the bay."

"And?" Winnie asked pointedly.

"And what?" Grandmother said as she unfolded her napkin and put it on her lap.

"Grandmother!" Clare cried. "Are they going to be married?"

"Of course not," Grandmother said. "She can't marry anyone until she has graduated from medical school. But he seems content to wait and follow her wherever she goes. So we must be content, too."

Mr. Younger tapped his glass with his spoon and called out from the parlor, "Have we had enough romance for one evening? I would like to hear about Hawaii, Mrs. Devereaux. Tell us everything."

He sounded grouchy, but then he always did. There was no trace in his voice of envy or sorrow. Clare held this thought as if it were a gold coin.

A new boarder joined them in May. Mr. Perry McBride, a long-time friend of Mr. Partridge, moved in and took Mr. Reynolds' place at the bridge table in the evenings.

"He seems like a nice old fellow," Mr. Younger observed after Clare finished reading the paper to him that afternoon. "Jackie says he has a small beard, and we both like that idea."

"My, my, aren't you feeling benevolent these days," Clare said as she folded the paper and got to her feet.

"I'm in a good mood," he said. "Jackie asked me to

take Tip for a walk alone, which astonished both the dog and me."

"It surprises me, too," Clare said. She looked out the window, wondering if Jackie and Tip were on the porch, but they were nowhere in sight. "But lately, he doesn't seem to want the company of anyone."

Mr. Younger was quiet for a moment, and then he said, "I've noticed that, too. We must keep an eye on him."

"Do you think he's ill?" Clare asked.

"No. I think he misses his father."

"But that's ridiculous," Clare argued. "Why would he miss a man who beat him black and blue and nearly cost him his eyesight?"

"He's Jackie's father," Mr. Younger said. "If you have only one parent, you can't afford to pick and choose. You, young miss, have two parents, so you are free to despise your father. Certainly, he was inadequate in every possible way. But you have a fine mother. Think how you'd feel if all you had was your father. And then try to imagine how you would feel if you were Jackie's age. To him, a bad father is better than none at all."

Clare stared at him. "How do you know all these things?"

He made a wry face. "You may have noticed that I'm not terribly busy, so I have time to think."

He was looking directly at her, the bright afternoon sun shining through the window on his face.

"What are you wearing?" he asked quietly. He was leaning forward a little, as if he were anxious about her answer.

After a long pause, she said, "My white dress."

He leaned back and the tension left his shoulders.

His sight is coming back, she thought suddenly. It's been coming back for a long time, even before he and his mother went to New York.

She hurried away before he guessed that she was smiling.

On Saturday at the Neighborhood House, little Grace caught Clare alone in the storeroom and tugged at her cardigan. "Jackie's Pa is back," she said.

Clare whirled around. "What?"

"He's back at the house," Grace said.

"Do you know if he's staying?" Clare asked. "Does he have a job?"

Grace shook her head. "No, Miss. He told my ma that he was going to Montana this summer."

"Did he say anything about Jackie?" Clare asked quickly.

Grace shook her head again. "Ma asked him did he

want to get his boy back, and he said 'What boy?' and laughed."

Clare was relieved and disgusted at the same time. How could he not want his child back? But what if he did? Jackie had a good life now.

But she remembered what Mr. Younger had told her about bad parents.

She told Grandmother and Winnie that Mr. Atherton was back, and she repeated what Grace had said. They, too, were disgusted that the man did not want his child.

"But this is a reason to celebrate," Winnie said. "If he's lost interest in Jackie, then we can stop worrying about his showing up sometime and making trouble."

The next morning, when Clare went downstairs to set the table for Sunday breakfast, Mrs. Klacker told her that Tip was in the kitchen, curled up in his box.

"Isn't that strange?" she said. "That's where he runs when Jackie leaves for school. Poor little dog has his days mixed up."

Clare turned and ran back upstairs. She threw open Jackie's door, and saw that his bed had been neatly made, the way she had taught him. His glasses lay on his desk, next to a note.

I am going back to my father. Mr. Younger can keep Tip. I do not need glasses now. Thank you for the food and clothes.

Jack Atherton

P.S. Please do not forget to feed Tip. He is a good boy.

15

Clare called Grandmother, Winnie, and Mama and told them Jackie was gone.

"How did he know his father was back?" Winnie asked. "We certainly didn't tell him. And he never goes near the Neighborhood House."

Grandmother hurried to the kitchen to question Mrs. Klacker. "Has a stranger been here, looking for Jackie?" she asked.

"Nobody's come looking for Jackie," Mrs. Klacker declared. "I would have said so right away. The only stranger I've seen was the man looking for yard work, but I told him that we had a handyman who took care of everything. You wouldn't have wanted him around anyway. He was an awfully dirty fellow. And he smelled as if he'd been drinking."

"Was Jackie here? Did Jackie see him?" Winnie asked.

Mrs. Klacker's broad face turned red. "Oh, God save me," she cried. "Jackie was right behind me in the hall, but as soon as Tip started barking — you know how he acts when he doesn't like someone — Jackie picked him up and took him upstairs."

"That was no stranger," Grandmother said.

"What have I done?" Mrs. Klacker wept.

Winnie put her arms around Mrs. Klacker. "Don't blame yourself. The only one to blame is Jackie's father."

As soon as the women dressed, they left for Atherton's old shack. But it was empty. Winnie's acquaintance across the street said that Atherton had left the evening before with all his belongings tied up in a cardboard box. He did not have the boy with him.

"Then he met him somewhere," Grandmother said. "I'm afraid we're too late."

"I'll see the social worker tomorrow," Winnie declared.

"It won't do any good," Mama said. "They have their hands full with the homeless children living in the alleys downtown. Jackie's with his father, and probably on his way out of the state by now."

"I can at least try," Winnie said.

But her efforts were useless. The social workers were appalled that Jackie was missing. Someone would visit the shack. Someone else would make a report. They would keep in touch.

When Winnie, defeated, came home with that news, Clare realized for the first time that the woman was old and becoming frail. How much longer could she continue to battle for helpless children? How much longer could Grandmother go on?

Sarah still came to the house on Saturday mornings for her chess lesson, and after the first time, she never again asked about Jackie. But she always spent a few minutes with Tip, holding him in her lap and stroking him.

"I'm sure Jackie is all right," Clare told her once, thinking that she might be worried about her friend.

Sarah nodded dutifully, but Clare knew she did not believe her.

The school's graduation ceremony was held on a bright June day in the gardens behind the refectory. Everyone from the boarding house attended. Clare missed Bonnie, who had written that she was still not well enough to enjoy the thought of traveling again so soon, but Bonnie had sent a thin gold bracelet that Clare wore to the ceremony.

The girls were dressed in white, and each carried a small bouquet of white flowers. Most of them had short hair now.

"I'll bet that every girl here is wearing a brassiere,"

Marietta whispered to Clare as they stood in line waiting to be given their diplomas.

"Hush," Clare said. "We don't want to miss it when our names are called."

"I can't hush," Marietta said. "We're on our way, Clare. We're actually on our way."

Clare's name was called then and she stepped forward. Everyone from the boarding house clapped when she accepted the stiff piece of paper.

Now what? Clare wondered as she returned to her seat. Now what will happen to me?

When the ceremony was over, Clare and Marietta joined the rest of their classmates at a garden party given by the parents of one of the girls. Clare suspected that she was the only one who was not having a good time. All the rest had made plans. Some would go on to college. One was marrying the son of her father's best friend in three weeks. Two girls were leaving for Europe immediately, and would not return for a year. And Marietta had confided to Clare that she had found her mother's "door slamming" money, concealed in a thin mesh bag pinned inside the sleeve of her old alpaca coat.

"I'm taking it all and leaving the day after my birthday," Marietta had told her.

"You can't do that," Clare had protested.

"I must, Clare," Marietta said. "I'll find a place to live

in New York and a job, too, and then, someday, I'll send for Sarah."

Clare stared at her. "But —" she began.

"If I don't rescue her, I don't know what will happen to her," Marietta said. "She's so unhappy. Now that Jackie's gone, she doesn't have a single friend. And Pa, well, he's getting meaner. It's something I have to do."

Clare thought that Marietta had courage, to make plans like that. And look at the plans Bonnie had made, and the adventures she had had! Yes, some were terrible. But still, she had taken charge of her life, as Marietta appeared to be doing.

I'm only floundering, Clare thought. I can't find answers to any of my questions.

That evening after dinner, Mr. Younger called Clare into his parlor. "You must begin writing in your journal tonight," he said. "And I hope this will make it easier." He reached out to give her a small package. She unwrapped it and found a slim silver pen with several gold pen points and a small silver inkpot.

"It's beautiful," she said. "Thank you."

"Now, what will you write tonight?" he asked.

She laughed a little. "I'll write that I don't know what to write, and I don't know what to do."

"You'll go to college," he said.

"There's no money," she said. "I'm certain that there isn't. Grandmother insists that she will manage, but I don't see how she can. I even wrote to my father, but he never answered."

"If you want to go, you shall," Mr. Younger said. "It would be my pleasure —"

"No!" Clare cried. "Don't go on, please. Don't even say it. I must find my own way there, if I'm to go at all. And who's to say that college is where I should be? I don't know what I want to do."

"I remember that you once wanted to learn to cook," Mr. Younger said. He was laughing at her.

"And you said I could learn from Mrs. Klacker. Well I am, when Grandmother and Winnie aren't home."

"Are you responsible for the gravy we had last night?" he demanded.

Clare scowled. "Yes. What of it?"

"I thought I recognized the Devereaux family touch," he said. "I remember when there was no cook in the kitchen and only Bonnie had the faintest idea of how to prepare a meal. The gravy stuck to the roofs of our mouths. And it was quite terrible last night, if you don't mind my saying so —"

"I do mind!" Clare said. "Why must you be so rude?"

"As I was saying before you interrupted me," Mr.

Younger went on placidly, "it was quite terrible, but I'm certain that Mrs. Klacker can help you improve. So when you have learned to cook, then what?"

"Then I'll teach a cooking class to the girls at the Neighborhood House. And I want to teach them to make dresses for themselves, and clothes for the other children in the family. And I want to show them how to make a bed properly, and scrub a kitchen and bathroom, and—"

"Good god," Mr. Younger said. "You're not going to make a career out of the Neighborhood House, are you?"

Clare was silent for a moment. "I can't," she said. "They don't pay anything. I'd like to do what Grandmother and Winnie have done, but I must find a job."

"Doing what?" Mr. Younger demanded.

Clare sighed. "That's just it. I don't know how to do anything. But there are places where one can learn to type."

"My god," Mr. Younger groaned. "You want to be shut up in an office all day?"

"Not especially," Clare said. "But it's out of the question anyway, because I won't have money for training."

"Then you'll have to find a husband," Mr. Younger said evenly. "That's what other girls do."

"I'm not other girls," Clare said. "I won't marry someone just because I can't take care of myself. Anyway, I don't know anyone to marry except boys from the tea dances at school, and I certainly wouldn't marry one of them, not even if he asked."

"Well, then, we have a problem," Mr. Younger said. "I expect I have my work cut out for me. As soon as you've learned to cook and sew, let me know and I'll ask around among my acquaintances and see if any of them would like a young, pretty wife. You are pretty, aren't you?"

Clare's face was flushed with annoyance and her hands clenched in fists. "If you took off your dark glasses, you probably could see well enough for yourself to judge whether or not I am. If it really makes a difference."

He sat as if frozen. And then he slowly removed his glasses.

She saw first that his eyes were green, flecked with gold, and then that his lashes were dark and very long.

They stared at one another for a long moment.

"I knew you were pretty," he said. "You left your hair long. I knew that, too. I saw you drying it in the sunshine on the side porch once."

Clare only looked at him.

"I don't see very well yet. Perhaps I never shall. But the doctors in New York agreed that it was possible I could regain enough sight so that I might read books and find my way about, even when the light isn't bright.

But for now, I can only see a little in very bright light, and you are the one I look for at those times."

Clare began to speak, stopped, and then began again. "You always wanted to know what I wore."

"Yes. After a while I could sometimes see for myself, but I wanted to make certain."

"Does anyone else know?"

"Jackie," he said. "He guessed one day when I was watching you sitting outside reading."

"I wonder where he is and how he is," she said sadly.

"And if he's having crackers and jam," Mr. Younger said. He put his dark glasses back on. "My eyes get tired," he explained.

"Are you going to tell the others?" Clare asked.

He shook his head. "No. I'm afraid of failing."

"Put a bell on the tree," Clare said, quite seriously.

"I did. I've tied three bells to the tree."

"You'd better not tell me any more," Clare said. "Your wishes won't come true."

He laughed. "You're quite right. I won't ask about yours, either. But from the sound of it, this household is keeping the tree busy."

True to her word, the day after her birthday Marietta disappeared. She left a brief note for her mother, another for Sarah, and nothing at all for her father. When the Nelsons came to the boarding house to ask Clare what she knew about Marietta's running away, Clare could truthfully tell them that they knew more than she, since Marietta had at least written to them.

"I wish she had said good-bye to me," Clare said.

Mr. Nelson turned on his heel and left without a word, but Mrs. Nelson dabbed at her eyes with a handkerchief and said, "Are you sure she never said anything to you about this? You were her best friend."

"I knew she didn't want to be married," Clare said.

"But what else could she do?" Mrs. Nelson asked, truly bewildered.

"Get a job or go to college," Clare said.

Mrs. Nelson flapped her tiny handkerchief. "What nonsense. I wish I'd never let Marietta make friends with you. She picked up all those crazy ideas here. Votes for women! Jobs for women! Other things I won't dignify by repeating. This is all your fault, Clare. Yours and your grandmother's. And Winnie's!"

She left then, wailing, and ran up the street after her husband.

Clare, who was alone in the house, wandered about restlessly for a few minutes, thinking of all the things she should have said to Marietta's mother and had not. What would the woman have thought if she learned of

Marietta's plans to take Sarah away? There were unpleasant parallels between Mr. Nelson and Jackie's awful father. Poor little Sarah. Apparently wealth did not protect a child from abuse.

What would make a difference in children's lives? Clare could not imagine. Should not a man be proud to be a father and want to do everything he could to make the child's life easy?

Apparently that was not the case. Then the solution had to be within the child. Children must learn to take care of themselves.

And so must I, Clare thought.

She changed her dress and smoothed her hair, then picked up her new pocketbook and walked briskly to the library where her mother worked.

"Clare, darling," Mama said when she saw her approach the desk. "I didn't know you were coming by today. Are you interested in seeing the new novels that came in?"

"No," Clare said. "I'm interested in the position the library advertised in the newspaper. The position of clerk. Oh yes, I saw it. I've been reading the help-wanted ads every morning."

Mama stared at her. "But Clare, you can't do that," she said in a lowered voice, even though no one stood near them. "It's a permanent position, dear, not summer work. You'll be entering college in the fall."

"Mama, you know there's no money for that," Clare said.

"Your grandmother is going to sell her pearls," Mama whispered. "We were keeping that as a surprise."

The pearls were beautiful, and meant for Mama when Grandmother died. Clare shook her head stubbornly. "No. This is something I must do for myself. I want a job, and you know I meet all the qualifications that were set out in the paper."

"But you wouldn't be a librarian," Mama said. "You'd only be an assistant, a clerk."

"I know. And when I've saved enough money, I'll go to college and maybe I'll study to be a librarian. But in the meantime, I must take care of myself."

"But your grandmother and Winnie will never approve," Mama said. Her eyes had filled with tears.

"I'll find work somewhere, or you'll leave me no choice but to go off on my own, the way Marietta did."

Mama pressed her fingers against her lips for a moment. "All right, then. All right. We've had two applicants so far, and you'll have to see Mr. Bain at the downtown branch because he's the one who gives the final interview. I can't ask for special favors for you, Clare. It wouldn't be fair."

"I know, Mama," Clare said. "Thank you. I'll tell

Grandmother and Winnie as soon as I see them."

"They'll have fits," Mama said.

Clare grinned. "At least I'm not going to China."

A letter came from Marietta in August.

I've found a job working as the assistant to the assistant bookkeeper in a factory that makes mattresses. It sounds horrible, doesn't it? But I like the girls I work with, and we have fun. I stayed in a small hotel for a few days when I first arrived, but then I found a room in a boarding house. It's not as nice as yours, and the food is terrible, but it's cheap. I'll get a raise soon, and be making thirty dollars a month. I wrote to my family and told them where I am, because I didn't want them to worry. I'm too far away for them to do anything about it. At least I don't have to get married.

All my love, Marietta

Clare began working at the library and walked back and forth with her mother every day. "Your grandmother is taking this very well," Mama remarked one day in September.

"If that's what you call it, now that she only tells me once a day that I'm ruining my life," Clare said, laughing.

"She and Winnie think you will grow tired of putting books back on shelves and agree to start college after Christmas," Mama said.

"No, Mama," Clare said.

"Bonnie will be starting medical school next fall," Mama said. "She's almost assured of getting in."

"She's a heroine, and after that San Francisco newspaper printed the article about her, I imagine no medical school would dream of turning her away," Clare said. "But I'm not Bonnie. I'm just plain Clare who wants to find a way to work at the Neighborhood House without starving to death while she's doing it."

"You won't starve," her mother chided. "But think what you could offer if you had the special training you'd receive at the university."

"What special training?" Clare said. "Would someone there teach me to scrub the bathroom? That's the sort of things the girls there need to learn. They have to be able to take care of themselves."

"Oh, dear, are you going to deliver that self-reliance lecture again?" Mama asked.

"As many times as I need to do it," Clare said cheerfully.

After dinner, Mr. Younger tapped on his glass and Clare went into the parlor carrying the newspaper, thinking that was what he wanted. He had been late coming home, and no one had read the headlines to him yet.

"Are you responsible for the gravy we had tonight?" he asked as she sat down on the sofa. Tip had made himself comfortable in Mr. Younger's lap, and wagged his tail lazily.

"I am indeed, and I thought it was quite fine," she answered.

"You're right," he said. "It was as good as anything Mrs. Klacker ever made."

"Then what made you think it was mine?" Clare asked.

"You left out the pepper." He scratched Tip's ears and patted him.

"Oh, I didn't!" she said.

"That's all right," he said. "Especially since Mrs. Klacker told me that you prepared most of the meal yourself, before your grandmother and Miss Devereaux got home."

"Don't tell them!" Clare said. "They have enough to bear right now."

"Your job," he said.

"It's a sore spot for them."

"Mrs. Carver told me she saw you in the library the other day, helping two scruffy little girls find books. She said you looked happy."

"Those were girls from the Neighborhood House. I've been encouraging them to read more than what they're given at school."

"You're enthusiastic about helping the children there, aren't you?"

"I can't forget Jackie," she said. "I can't help him directly anymore, but when I'm working with the others, I like to think that somewhere someone is helping him."

Mr. Younger was silent for a moment, and then he said, "You are what people mean when they say someone is good through and through."

Clare laughed disrespectfully. "That's not what you would have said when you first met me."

"As I recall, the day I met you, you had just been caught stealing ice from the ice wagon."

"That was the day Bonnie came to live with us," Clare said. "So much has happened since then."

"We've had our adventures," he said. He took off his

dark glasses and put them on the table next to him. "Come and sit here with Tip and me," he said.

She put down the newspaper and sat on the ottoman in front of him. "Are you seeing better these days?" she asked.

"Well enough," he said. "I saw the doctor downtown this afternoon. He told me that with glasses, I might manage quite nicely for a few hours each day."

"I'm so glad!" she said. "Then are you going to tell the others?"

"I thought I'd surprise them," he said. "I get my glasses next week — they'll be even thicker than Jackie said his were — and I thought I might just walk in on everybody. I think I can tell one from the other, but I'm counting on you to help me."

"Oh, with anything!" she said. She leaned forward and took his hands. "This is wonderful. Aren't you excited?"

"I wanted to dance in the street after I heard, but I was afraid I'd be arrested, and you know how your grandmother would feel about that. She wouldn't think I was at all suitable for you if I had a jail record."

Clare's smile froze on her face. Then she pulled her hands free of his and buried her face in them.

"Now what?" he asked. "You aren't having one of those Victorian attacks of the vapors, are you? I know it was all the rage twenty-five years ago to blush and faint away when a man declared his intentions, but surely you are a modern young woman. Especially coming from this house."

Clare lowered her hands. "I'm not sure what you're asking — or telling me," she said.

"Of course you're sure, you exasperating little beast. You know how I've felt about you since you put up your hair. I've discussed it all with Tip, and he's quite enthusiastic about everything, even the wait while you make up your mind about what else you want to do with your life."

Clare held out her hands and he took them again. "I don't know what Mama and Grandmother will think about this," she said.

"But you and I are the ones whose opinions matter most," he said. "Now, dear heart, what ghastly news does the paper hold for us this evening?"

Clare brought the paper back to the ottoman and leaned against the arm of his chair while she read. Outside, a warm September wind stirred the bells in the tree.

Two hundred miles away, a small boy had curled himself up to sleep in the back of a stranger's farm wagon. He was traveling alone toward Seattle. He carried all of his belongings in a sack, including a penny, a book with stories about horses, a small dog collar he had fashioned out of a discarded bit of harness, and a bell he had made from a scrap of tin. While he slept, he smiled.